Dinah for President

By Claudia Mills

HANNAH ON HER WAY

DYNAMITE DINAH

AFTER FIFTH GRADE, THE WORLD!

CALLY'S ENTERPRISE

THE ONE AND ONLY CYNTHIA JANE THORNTON

BOARDWALK WITH HOTEL

Claudia Mills

Dinah for President

Macmillan Publishing Company   New York
Maxwell Macmillan Canada   Toronto
Maxwell Macmillan International
New York   Oxford   Singapore   Sydney

Printed in the United States of America

3   5   7   9   10   8   6   4   2

The text of this book is set in 12 pt. Sabon.

Library of Congress Cataloging-in-Publication Data

Mills, Claudia. Dinah for president / Claudia Mills. — 1st ed.   p.   cm.

Summary: Dinah Seabrooke, now in her first year of middle school, struggles to become a big fish in what seems like an ocean—and in the process discovers the value of recycling and of friendship with the elderly.

ISBN 0-02-766999-8

[1. Schools—Fiction.   2. Elections—Fiction.   3. Recycling (Waste)—Fiction.   4. Old age—Fiction.]   I. Title.   PZ7.M63963Di 1992   [Fic]—

dc20   91-34839

For Gregory

Dinah for President

One

WELCOME, DINAH SEABROOKE!

The greeting filled the huge sign set on the front lawn of John F. Kennedy Middle School. Actually, the big white letters spelled out WELCOME, STUDENTS!, but Dinah couldn't help thinking the message was meant for her personally. After all, it was her first day ever of middle school, and it was the middle school's first day ever of Dinah.

"This is it," Dinah said to her best friend, Suzanne Kelly, who had followed her down the steps of the school bus. Dramatically, she recited one of her mother's favorite sayings, "Today is the first day of the rest of our lives."

"Don't *say* that." Suzanne groaned. "The first day of school is bad enough. I just hope we have some classes together. And that we don't get lost trying to find them. Or miss our bus going home."

Dinah certainly hoped for more than *that*. She wanted excitement. She wanted adventure. She wanted undying fame.

"How will we know which bus is ours?" Suzanne went on. "What if we take the wrong one?"

"What if we *do*? Maybe we'll get on a better bus, one that will be hijacked by pirates—or cannibals! Or, okay, not pirates or cannibals." Dinah forced herself to be realistic. "But it could be bank robbers. Or terrorists. Anyway, we'll outwit them somehow and save the day, and afterward we'll be interviewed on the evening news. On all three networks."

Suzanne laughed. "I guess we'd just get off somewhere and call my mother and she'd come and get us. But I hope it doesn't happen, all the same."

The two girls joined the crowd of students waiting outside the doors of the middle school. Dinah stuck out her tongue at Artie Adams, whom she knew from fifth grade. But for every face she recognized, there seemed to be a hundred strangers, talking and laughing with their friends just the way she was talking and laughing with Suzanne. To them, Dinah could have been *anybody*. They didn't know that her nickname was Dynamite Dinah and that the first and second graders in her elementary school had nudged each other in awestruck silence when she'd walked by.

"Look how big the eighth graders are," Suzanne said in a low voice. "Some of those boys must be six feet tall. And the girls look like they're practically twenty, don't you think?"

It was odd being the little ones, after having been the big ones just two-and-a-half months before. And it was odd being nobody, when just two-and-a-half months before, Dinah had been somebody. Suddenly Dinah found herself hoping she *would* have lots of classes with Suzanne, and not get lost in the middle school's mazelike hallways. She even hoped her bus wouldn't get hijacked by terrorists for another week or two.

The bell rang. The solid steel doors of JFK Middle School swung open, and Dinah was carried inside with the pushing, shoving surge of students. Where was her homeroom? Dinah tried to remember from the orientation session last spring: upstairs, to the left. But where were the stairs? She turned to ask Suzanne, but Suzanne had disappeared into the crowd. Then she saw the school's central staircase, right where it had been in June. But in June there hadn't been a horde of stampeding giants, ready to trample a lost little sixth grader to death.

Safe in her homeroom at last, Dinah took a seat near the door, the better to make a quick getaway to her first class. In fifth grade, Dinah had once climbed out a classroom window onto the school roof, but the middle school classrooms had no windows. No more gazing out at the lazy drift of falling leaves, no more running to catch the first glimpse of swirling snow.

One by one, the other students straggled in, most looking as bewildered as Dinah felt. Dinah's homeroom teacher, Mrs. Vogel, a small middle-aged woman with a kind face, gave a reassuring smile to each in turn.

Mrs. Vogel was the math teacher, and the bulletin

board next to Dinah was labeled GREAT MATHEMATI-
CIANS. The yellowing pictures thumbtacked beneath
had obviously hung there for many years. Dinah con-
sidered hopping up and adding a trim little mustache
to Pythagoras, but it hardly seemed worth it. She con-
tented herself with sticking a spare thumbtack in the
middle of Sir Isaac Newton's nose.

Mrs. Vogel was too busy smiling to notice, but the
girl sitting across the aisle from Dinah gave her a
disapproving look. Hadn't she ever seen a great mathematician with a bright red thumbtack through his
nose?

"Isaac the red-nosed mathematician," Dinah said.
"He guides people's sleighs on Christmas Eve."

The girl didn't laugh. She was very pretty, with
every strand of her long, light-brown hair smoothly
in place. Dinah could tell just by looking at her that
this girl's crisp white blouse would never come un-
tucked from her skirt, and that her tights would never
dare to sag.

Dinah was about to put a yellow thumbtack in René
Descartes when the second bell rang. A man's voice
came booming over the school's public-address system: "Good morning. Please rise and salute the flag."
As the class stood, the voice led them through the
Pledge of Allegiance. Then it cleared its throat and
continued: "This is John Roemer, your principal."

In elementary school Dinah had been a frequent
visitor to the principal's office, so she listened closely,
trying to match a face to Mr. Roemer's hearty voice.

The principal made a few announcements, then said: "I hope all of you had a good summer and are returning this fall to JFK relaxed and refreshed. I must remind you, however, that *certain behaviors* that you may have found amusing during vacation are *not* acceptable here in the halls or on the grounds of JFK. I trust those of you to whom this reminder is addressed know what I'm talking about."

Dinah was curious. *What* behaviors? To whom *was* the message addressed? Would she ever do something remarkable enough that a morning announcement would be directed at her personally?

"Mooning," the boy sitting in front of Dinah said. He was tall for a sixth-grade boy, with broad, athletic-looking shoulders.

"What?" Dinah leaned forward to ask.

"Some of the eighth-grade guys were mooning out in front of the school when Roemer drove up this morning. He chased them, but they got away. That's what he's talking about."

"What's mooning?" the girl sitting across the aisle from Dinah asked, so that Dinah didn't have to.

Obviously the boy relished his role as know-it-all. "*You* know. Hanging a full one."

"A full *what*?"

"Moon. Don't you know anything? They bend over, drop their pants, and flash a big view of their behinds."

Dinah was shocked. She was used to being the center of attention, but never in a million billion years would it have occurred to her to pull down her *underwear* in public. But the boy had made it sound as if mooning, in middle school, were run-of-the-mill. It had to be fairly common if there was already a *word* for it. Where did that leave Dinah? If mooning was ordinary, what would count as extraordinary? Becoming the secret star of morning announcements at JFK Middle School was going to be harder than Dinah had thought.

The other girl flicked back her perfect hair. "That," she said, "is positively disgusting."

So about one thing, at least, she and Dinah agreed.

Mrs. Vogel passed out the schedule cards and locker keys. Dinah saw that she and the girl, whose name was Blaine Yarborough, had four of the same classes: English, math, social studies, and science. How many would Suzanne have? Suzanne, who would have looked at the thumbtack in Sir Isaac's nose and burst out laughing.

Another bell rang, this time to signal the end of homeroom. Apparently Dinah's whole life from now on was going to be guided by bells, bells, bells. On her way out the door, Dinah put the red thumbtack back where it belonged. Moving it had seemed funnier at the time than it did now.

To her relief, Dinah discovered that she and Suzanne had three classes together, as well as fifth-period lunch. They sat together during first period in English. Suzanne's eyes widened when Dinah explained to her the true meaning of Mr. Roemer's mysterious morning announcement.

"You're kidding!" she said. "They really did *that?*"

"It's called mooning," Dinah said, as if she had known about it for years. "People do it all the time in middle school."

"I don't think I like middle school," Suzanne confessed.

Dinah was sorry she had pretended to be an expert on mooning. "Me, neither," she whispered back.

As the morning progressed, Dinah began to think that the whole idea of middle school was a terrible mistake. In English class, Mr. Prensky passed out boring-looking grammar textbooks. Weren't they going to memorize poems? Or put on plays? Or learn language skills by editing a classroom newspaper?

Mr. Prensky adjusted his glasses before he answered Dinah's burst of questions. "Let me suggest that you attend the after-school activities fair next week," he said. "You may want to consider joining the Drama Club. Or signing up to work on the *JFK Herald*. Now, class, this morning we will begin our study of pronouns. Please turn to page five in *Fun with Grammar*."

Dinah got the message. In middle school, anything really fun was an *after*-school activity.

Certainly there was nothing fun about second-period gym.

Fweep! Miss Brady blew on her whistle. "Girls! Line yourselves up! You can stand up straighter than that!

Haven't you heard of something called *posture*? Come on, eyes front! Square those shoulders. You, Curly Top!" Was Miss Brady talking to Dinah? Dinah's short, dark hair was curly. But the teacher pounced on a girl toward the front of the line. "You, tuck in that tummy."

Then Miss Brady blew on her whistle again. "This morning I want to begin by explaining to you some of my class rules. Each of you is responsible for bringing to class appropriate gym wear and gym shoes. Failure to bring your gym wear to class, a zero for the day. Ditto, for gym shoes. Dirty gym wear, ten points off your grade for the week. Sneakers without laces, five points off your grade. You will have three minutes each day to change into your gym wear. Tardiness, ten points off your grade. Bring a combination lock from home to lock your gym lockers during class. Failure to lock your locker, five points off your grade. Forgetting the combination of your lock, five points."

Dinah fully expected Brady to continue the list: *Smiling, ten points off your grade; laughing, twenty points off your grade; showing any sign of enjoying yourself whatsoever, a zero for the day!*

"All right, girls, come forward one at a time for your locker assignments."

Fweep! Fweep! Dinah had been wrong: Her whole life wasn't going to be guided by bells. It was going to be guided by bells and whistles.

Science class third period looked more promising.

The science room had real lab tables, with real Bunsen burners and all kinds of magical-looking chemicals in bottles lined up along one wall. For math, fourth period, Dinah was back in her homeroom with Mrs. Vogel. She noticed a small hole in the middle of the picture where her thumbtack had been.

At last it was time for lunch. On her way to the cafeteria Dinah stopped at her locker outside Mrs. Vogel's room. Wearily, she stowed her three fat textbooks on the shelf.

Some of Mr. Roemer's announcements that morning had been about lockers. Students could hang pictures on the inside of their lockers, but there would be periodic locker inspections, and any unsuitable material would be removed. No food, weapons, or drugs could be stored in lockers. Lockers were to be kept neat and clean. No decoration of any kind could appear on the outside of any locker. No locker doors were to be slammed.

At that moment Dinah had had enough of JFK Middle School and its rules. She felt like putting a week-old tuna sandwich in her locker and a picture of—of someone *mooning* on the inside door. And on the outside door she'd write her name in big yellow letters with gold stars all around it: DINAH SEABROOKE'S LOCKER. KEEP OUT, WORLD! For emphasis, she slammed her locker door, loud and hard.

There!

Dinah would have felt much better—except that her skirt was caught in the locker door. And her key was on the little shelf inside, where she had left it right on top of *Fun with Grammar*.

Dinah tugged at her skirt, but she couldn't pull it free. "Hey!" she called to a guy whose locker was three doors down from hers, but he walked off without hearing. If only Suzanne would come by! But Suzanne's locker was far away.

Dinah had wanted to be a celebrity, but she didn't particularly want to be known as the girl who got her skirt stuck in her locker on the first day of school. And she didn't want to spend her whole lunch period starving in the hallway all by herself, when she could have been eating pizza with Suzanne.

"Excuse me!" Dinah called out, but the sixth graders rushed by, small and frightened-looking, and the seventh and eighth graders sauntered by, looking neither to the right nor to the left.

"Help!" Dinah tried, a little louder. She waved her arms. She put a thumb in each ear and wiggled her fingers. She sang the chorus from "The Battle Hymn of the Republic."

No one noticed. No one stopped.

Maybe in slamming the door she had somehow turned herself invisible. It might be interesting, being invisible, if she ever got herself free from her locker. But Dinah wasn't really the invisible type. She was the *visible* type. Or she had been until today.

"You're going to be late," a voice hissed in Dinah's ear. It was Blaine Yarborough, stopping at the locker next to hers. "I'm late, too, but I have a pass from

Miss Brady. I was helping her with the locker assignments last period."

Somehow that didn't surprise Dinah at all.

"I'm stuck." Dinah turned so Blaine could see her skirt, caught in the door.

"Where's your key?"

"In the locker."

Blaine clucked with exasperation. "Why did you leave it *there*?"

"I *didn't*. I mean, I didn't mean to. The door sort of slammed shut."

"We're not supposed to slam locker doors, you know. Remember what Mr. Roemer said this morning?"

Dinah glared at her. "Are you going to help me or not?"

"Of course I'll help you. I'll go get the master key from the main office."

Then Blaine was gone, off to the rescue.

So Dinah wasn't invisible, after all. Right then and there she vowed that JFK Middle School was going to find out just how invisible she wasn't. Somehow, someday, Dinah was going to make a mark on middle school, more than just a pinprick in Sir Isaac Newton's nose.

Two

That afternoon Dinah and Suzanne got off the bus together at Suzanne's house. "Which teacher did you hate the most?" Dinah asked Suzanne as they dropped their heavy backpacks onto a bench in the Kellys' big, old-fashioned kitchen and accepted hugs from Suzanne's mother. Mrs. Kelly was a church organist and music director, so she was often home in the afternoons.

"Miss Brady," Suzanne said promptly. "What about you?"

"Brady, I guess. Not that Prensky was exactly a barrel of laughs. Or Mr. Dixon in social studies, either. You don't have him, right? Well, Dixon talks too loud, and he calls kids by their last names, to sound tough or something. I think he tries to copy that guy on TV—you know, the one who talks about current events, and shouts at everybody, and acts like he knows everything?"

"Mr. Dixon should marry Miss Brady," Suzanne

suggested. "Unless he's already married. It might make Brady nicer if she had somebody."

Dinah didn't see how being married to Mr. Dixon could make anybody *nicer*, but lately Suzanne had been saying and doing a number of odd things. Like pointing out cute boys, and checking out *Abby in Love* three times in a row from the teen section in the public library. Dinah didn't mind, exactly, except—well, she couldn't have Suzanne, of all people, turning into a *teenager* right before her eyes. And Dinah had already decided that she herself was never going to be in love with any boy.

"Which teacher did you *like* the most?" Mrs. Kelly asked, setting a plate of molasses cookies on the long oak table.

"Miss McKay," both girls said together. The home economics teacher—pretty and good-natured—was everybody's favorite.

Suzanne's older brother Tom, a high school junior, bounded into the kitchen and reached for a handful of cookies. "Dynamite!" he greeted Dinah. "Have they renamed JFK yet in your honor?"

"No," Dinah said. "So far it's been kind of . . . the opposite, really." She told the Kellys her story.

"Give it a week," Tom advised her. "These things take time." He grabbed a second handful of cookies and was gone.

A week! A year would be more like it. But Tom's teasing made Dinah feel better. So did the molasses cookies, soft and gingery, still warm from the oven.

Dinah took a cookie home with her when she left, for her brother, Benjamin. Benjamin was six months old and just starting to eat solid food. So far he hated every mouthful of it. As soon as he saw his little blue ABC bowl and little silver teddy bear spoon, he clamped his mouth shut and screwed up his face to cry. Dinah hardly blamed him. Who would want to eat thin, gray rice cereal mixed with lukewarm baby formula? If her parents wanted Benjamin to eat solid food, they were going to have to give him some solid food worth eating. A homemade molasses cookie, for example.

"Benjamin!" Dinah called from the front hallway. "Cookie time!"

She half expected him to come running down the stairs, shouting, "Cookie! Cookie! Cookie!" But Benjamin couldn't even crawl, let alone walk. He couldn't talk, except for coos and gurgles. He didn't even know what a cookie *was*, poor little guy. But Dinah loved him, anyway.

"Yoo-hoo! Benjamin!" Then Dinah remembered: Her mother was starting back to work this week, and Benjamin was at his first day ever of day care, at Mrs. Haywood's house three blocks away. Dinah wondered if Benjamin had liked day care any better than she had liked middle school.

A few minutes later Dinah heard her mother's car in the driveway. She ran outside to give Benjamin a big welcome-home hug.

"How was school, honey?" Dinah's mother joined in the embrace.

"It was okay. How was work? How did Benjamin do at day care?"

"He loved it." Dinah couldn't tell if her mother sounded relieved or a little bit disappointed. "It felt good to be working again, although one of my new clients is an absolute doozy. I'll tell you about her at dinner. School was okay? Not wonderful, not awful, just okay?"

"Well, more like awful, if you really want to know. Actually, more like hideous and horrible and horrendous."

In the kitchen, Dinah told her mother all about middle school as Benjamin leaped and soared in the jumper that hung in the doorway. He didn't seem any the worse for his hours at day care. Maybe it was easier to start something new when you were so new yourself. He wouldn't take a single nibble of Dinah's cookie, though. He refused to open his mouth for even one tiny crumb.

"It'll get better," Dinah's mother predicted when Dinah had poured out her tale of woe. "You're used to being a big frog in a little pond, and now you're a little frog in a big pond. That's a hard adjustment to make."

"Ribbet," Dinah croaked in agreement, and Benjamin laughed. He might not eat cookies yet, but he had a better sense of humor than Blaine Yarborough.

At dinner Dinah once again recounted the day's adventures and disappointments so that her father, home from his job at the sporting goods store, could hear them. Dinah's stories tended to improve with each telling, and this one was no exception.

"So when I get to school, the first thing I see is these boys *mooning* right there in front of the principal's office. Do you know what mooning is? That's right, and they did it right in front of everybody. And in gym class? We have this teacher named Miss Brady and she takes points off your grade for *everything*. She gave one kid twenty points off just for laughing. She really did. And I almost got ten points off for smiling, but when she asked me, 'You, Curly Top, what are you smiling at?' I said, 'Nothing, Miss Brady,' and I stuck a big frown on my face really fast. And then right before lunch I accidentally slammed my locker door, and it just so happened that my skirt was caught in it, and I couldn't get it open because the key was inside. Guess how long I had to stand there before someone rescued me. Two whole hours. I would have fainted, but I couldn't even keel over, because I was stuck in the door."

"Hold on to the movie rights for that one," her father said with a wink. He gave a few more cranks to Benjamin's windup swing. "What about you, little guy? Did you have a good time today at day care?"

"Da," Benjamin said, but it didn't mean anything in English. Despite his parents' coaxing, he hadn't eaten any real food for supper—just his usual bottle of baby formula and a single spoonful of the hated rice cereal.

Dinah's mother put down her fork. "My second client today gets the prize, I think, for *the* most disorganized person I've ever come across in all my years as an organization consultant. You know, usually people hire me because they want to organize something small and manageable: their filing system, an attic, a reception, a baby-sitting co-op. One man hired me once just to organize the glove compartment in his car. But Mrs. Briscoe needs her entire life organized. I mean it—the whole thing."

"You'd have to be fairly organized just to get around to hiring an organization consultant," Dinah's father said. "At least she has that in her favor."

"That's just it," Dinah's mother said. "She didn't hire me. Her daughter, Ruth, did. Ruth doesn't see how her mother can continue to cope all alone in that big house with so many stairs, but she's not in a position to have her mother move in with her. Basically, the alternatives are: I help Mrs. Briscoe to get her house organized in some livable way, or her daughter will have to put her into a retirement home."

"You still haven't said what's *wrong* with her," Dinah said. "She's disorganized, like how?"

"I hardly know where to start. Her house. It's—it's—Mrs. Briscoe is eighty-two years old, and as far as I can tell she has never thrown away a single, solitary newspaper in all those years. Three-hundred-sixty-five newspapers a year, times sixty-odd years. Jerry, you're good at math. Help me. That's—"

"Over twenty thousand," Dinah's father supplied.

"Over twenty thousand newspapers. Stacked over half her living room. And the magazines, and the junk mail, decades worth of it." Dinah's mother shook her head. "Her kitchen. The shelves are crammed, just crammed, with food that's been there goodness knows how long. I saw a box of macaroni that had an address on it so old it didn't have a zip code. One kitchen drawer, absolutely groaning with jumbled silverware and utensils, was hanging open and about to fall out any minute, and what was perched on top of it? An enormous butternut squash. Not that I saw any better place to put it, frankly."

"Can't you just empty the contents of her house into one big dumpster?" Dinah's father asked.

"*One* dumpster? A hundred dumpsters would be more like it. The regular garbage collectors won't make a bulk pickup like that. I guess I'll try to contact a recycling center about the papers, at least. But there's still going to have to be a lot of sifting and sorting. It's not as if she were dead, and the only goal were to get rid of her stuff. We have to clear a space for her to *live* in. That's the challenge."

"You still haven't told us what she's like," Dinah said.

"You can see for yourself on Saturday. Congratulations, Dinah. You've just been hired as a junior partner in Seabrooke Organizing, Incorporated."

By Friday Dinah knew the halls of JFK Middle School so well that she could have found her way to her classes blindfolded. She was tempted to try it, just for fun. It would make a good headline in the *JFK Herald*: BLINDFOLDED SIXTH GRADER ASTONISHES ALL. But she had a sinking feeling that even if she did wear a blindfold to school one day, nobody would notice. So far, nobody even knew her *name*. In English class, Mr. Prensky kept calling her Denise for some reason. In gym class, she was one of the four or five girls Miss Brady called Curly Top. In social studies, Mr. Dixon got her last name right, but he had to check his seating chart every time before he bellowed it out. Little frog in a big pond? Dinah felt like a tadpole adrift in the Atlantic Ocean.

So Dinah was glad when Saturday came, even if she was supposed to spend most of the day helping her mother organize Mrs. Briscoe.

Mrs. Briscoe's house was a tall, narrow Victorian, yellow with white trim, on a corner lot near the public library. From the outside it looked like anybody else's house, except that the yard was overgrown with dandelions and a riot of wildflowers.

"Believe me, the weeds are the least of our problems," Dinah's mother said in a low voice.

Mrs. Briscoe opened the door to their knock. She was a tiny, birdlike woman with bright, shy eyes.

"Come in, come in!" she said. "It's so kind of you both to take all this trouble with me, Mrs. Seabrooke and—it's Dinah, isn't it? Do come in." Mrs. Briscoe took hold of Dinah's hand and gave it a soft squeeze. "Let me make you some tea, if I can find the teapot. My kitchen is a bit cluttered right now, I'm afraid. But, then, that's what you're here to take care of, isn't it?"

Still holding Dinah's hand, Mrs. Briscoe led them down the dark hallway, lined on either side with cardboard cartons stacked three high.

"I know I saw the teapot last week," Mrs. Briscoe said when they had reached the kitchen. "I have another one—somewhere—but this one I particularly like. It's shaped like a frog—a big, fat old bullfrog. Do you like frogs, Dinah? I must say, I'm terribly fond of them. You must let me show you my frog collection if we have time. It's so nice having company. I usually don't, you know. Now, the teapot. I suppose I could brew the tea in a saucepan. But we'll need cups, too, of course, and it's been so long since I—Dinah, tell me, if you were a frog teapot, where would you be?"

It was such an odd question Dinah hardly knew how to answer. She wasn't a frog teapot, and if she were, she'd be on the stove, where Mrs. Briscoe's teapot obviously wasn't. If she were a butternut squash she would be in the refrigerator, yet she saw the squash her mother had mentioned, still sitting in the open silverware drawer.

"We don't need any tea," Dinah's mother said quickly. "There's so much to be done, I think we'd better just begin right away."

"It may turn up," Mrs. Briscoe said. "Things generally do. Just the other day I found a pair of eyeglasses that I'd been looking for for weeks, and guess where they were? In their case, in my pocketbook! The last place I thought of looking, I must say. You're sure about the tea? It would really be no trouble."

"We're sure," Dinah's mother said. "But perhaps we should begin in the kitchen. It's as good a place as any."

"Oh, if you *would*," Mrs. Briscoe said. "And, please, be ruthless! Do whatever you need to do. Ruth told me—very sternly—that I'm to cooperate with you both to the fullest. In fact, I'll tiptoe away right now and let you surprise me with all your progress. Just— Well, one little thing. I wouldn't want you to throw anything *away*. Not without checking with me first."

Dinah glanced over at her mother. What about the hundred dumpsters?

"Mrs. Briscoe," Dinah's mother said gently, "we *have* to throw things away. Ninety percent of our job is going to be to throw things away."

Mrs. Briscoe's chin trembled. "I'm sorry, but, no, I really can't have you discarding anything. I have letters, mementos, so many things that— You're young, both of you. You have no idea what my things *mean* to me."

"We won't throw away a single letter," Dinah's mother said. "We'll get rid of only what we truly need to. You have my word on that. Now, why don't you go rest in the living room, and Dinah and I will get to work."

"I suppose it's for the best," Mrs. Briscoe said with apparent effort. "I do want to stay here if I can, without being a burden to Ruth or anyone." She gave a quick, uncertain smile, and turned to go.

"All right, Dinah," her mother said when they were alone, "run to the car and get the box of trash bags. I'm sure we'll need at least a dozen for the kitchen."

Slowly, Dinah obeyed. Life was so full of changes: changes for her, changes for Benjamin, changes for Mrs. Briscoe. Dinah didn't approve of any of them. What was so terrible about having a squash in your silverware drawer? Why did Benjamin have to eat solid food if he didn't want to? Why couldn't Dinah still be a big famous frog in her old familiar pond?

Three

Mr. Roemer had a habit of clearing his throat every day before he began reading the morning announcements. By the end of another week of school, the students in Dinah's homeroom had learned to make a loud chorus of exaggerated throat-clearing sounds as soon as the public-address system clicked on.

Except for Blaine. "He *is* the principal," Blaine said across the aisle to Dinah on Friday. "He deserves a little respect."

"Urgh!" Dinah replied. "Ack-ack-aahgh!"

It was fun making the noises, even if it hadn't been her idea, even if everyone else was doing it, too. In fact, Dinah was having such a good time clearing her throat that she almost missed the first announcement of the day.

"Petitions for class office are due here on my desk next Tuesday," Mr. Roemer read. "There are four class offices: president, vice president, secretary, and treasurer. You may pick up petitions in the library or in the front office. Twenty signatures are needed to put your name on the ballot. Elections will take place on Friday, October fourth, with a runoff election the following week if necessary.

"This afternoon all students are urged to stay until four-thirty for the activities fair. Special buses will take you home afterward. . . ."

Dinah tuned out, even though she had been looking forward to the activities fair all week, waiting for the moment when she could join the JFK Drama Club. The middle school put on long plays at night—not short plays during school assemblies, as Dinah's elementary school had done. Dinah hoped that even though she was a sixth grader, the drama coach would give her the lead in a play. She imagined the billboard: HAMLET, STARRING DINAH SEABROOKE. Dinah didn't know what *Hamlet* was about, but her father had told her it was the most famous play ever written. She even knew the most famous line from this most famous play: "To be, or not to be, that is the question." She practiced saying it in front of her bedroom mirror sometimes.

Now *Hamlet* was forgotten. *President Dinah*. She liked the sound of it—a big-frog kind of sound. If a class president accidentally caught her skirt in her locker, other people would *do* something about it. Dinah could picture her first press conference, the reporters shouting their questions as the TV cameras whirred. *"Excuse me, Madam President!"* Would the middle school marching band play "Hail to the Chief" when she made her appearance at school sporting events? Probably not. But maybe they'd play the school song, "JFK for Me."

As soon as the bell rang, Dinah sprinted to the office for her petition. Breathless, she slid into her seat in English class just as the next bell rang.

"Here." She thrust her petition at Suzanne. "You can be the first to sign."

"Your petition? You got it already? What are you running for?"

"What do you think?"

Suzanne looked down at the petition. Over her shoulder, Dinah read the words at the top of the page once again: "We, the undersigned, hereby nominate Dinah Seabrooke for the office of sixth-grade president."

"President? The kids in my homeroom said the president's always a boy. The secretary's always a girl. Vice president and treasurer can be either one."

"Why *can't* a girl be president? Give me one good reason." *Besides*, Dinah added to herself, *I'm not any old girl.*

"You're right," Suzanne said. "There's no reason."

"You should run for something with me. How about vice president?"

"Well, I . . ."

Dinah had a horrible thought. What if Suzanne secretly wanted to be president, too? Dinah knew she tended to hog things sometimes. Suzanne had as much right to be the first girl president as she did.

"Or president." Dinah swallowed hard. "We can *both* run. And may the better girl win!"

"Are you kidding? I don't want to be president. You couldn't pay me to be president."

Thank you, universe, thank you! Dinah's heart sang.

"But I was thinking—well, it would be kind of fun to be secretary. I think I'd be a good secretary. My handwriting's really neat. See?" Suzanne opened her notebook for Dinah's inspection.

"You'd be a wonderful secretary," Dinah told her. "How about, I'll be your campaign manager and you can be mine? We'll make signs together at my house today. And buttons! And a great big banner—"

"Today's the activities fair," Suzanne reminded her.

"Well, this weekend, then. JFK has never *seen* a campaign like ours is going to be!"

By lunchtime Dinah had collected eighteen of her twenty signatures. It was easy getting the kids sitting near her in all her classes to sign. Only two refused. Artie Adams said flat out, "A *girl* can't be *president*."

"Why not?" Dinah demanded.

"Girls just aren't— Look, has there ever been a woman president of the United States? Answer me that."

"They didn't even let women *vote* for the first couple of hundred years," Dinah shot back. She knew she had the dates wrong, but the idea was right. Suddenly she wanted to be not only the first girl class president, but someday the first woman president of the entire USA.

"Girls are too emotional," Artie insisted.

Dinah resisted the urge to scream, "*I'm not too emotional! I'm not! I'm not!*" Instead she said, as calmly as she could, "It's your school. If you don't care about getting the best officers possible, regardless of race, sex, religion, or—emotionalness—then I feel sorry for you."

The other kid who didn't sign, a boy named Greg Thomas, asked Dinah, "What's your platform?"

"My platform?"

"What are you planning to do as president? What do you want to achieve? Are you going to try to get us more sports equipment? Or an extra class trip? Or less homework?"

Dinah had never thought about what she would *do* as president. She just wanted to *be* president.

"I have to think about it," she admitted.

The boy handed the petition back to her. "I'll sign it after you do," he said.

Dinah herself signed other kids' petitions for vice president and treasurer, as well as Suzanne's for class secretary. During sixth-period social studies, Jason Winfield, the boy in Dinah's homeroom who knew all about mooning, stuck his petition under her nose.

"Sign it," he commanded. "I'm running for president." His friendly grin took any offense out of the order. But he certainly seemed confident of being obeyed.

"Sorry," Dinah said sweetly. She waved her own petition back at him. "I'm running, too."

"Not for president."

"Yes, for president."

"You don't have a chance," Jason said, as if he were an expert on both mooning *and* elections.

Dinah refused to be impressed by his air of authority. "Says who?"

"Come on, Seabrooke. Get real," Jason said. "You're a girl. G-I-R-L."

"You can spell, Jason?" Dinah asked in mock surprise. "I didn't know boys could spell."

Jason punched her in the arm, not hard enough to hurt, but hard enough that Dinah jerked her arm away.

"It's your funeral, Seabrooke," he said cheerfully.

"How do you spell *funeral?*" Dinah asked him.

Jason's answer came quickly enough. "E-L-E-C-T-I-O-N."

The activities fair was held after school in the gym. Each club had a booth where students could find out about its activities and meet the teacher who served as club advisor. Dinah and Suzanne had both decided to join the Drama Club, but they walked by all the other booths, anyway.

"I thought about joining the school orchestra," Suzanne said, stopping by the music booth, "but I already spend so much time on my piano lessons that my parents thought I should branch out a little bit."

Suzanne played the piano better than any kid Dinah had ever heard—practically as well, Dinah thought, as the grown-ups who performed on the radio and TV. And even though she was shy compared to Dinah, Suzanne was a good actress, too. Last year, in fifth grade, Suzanne had played the best role in one class play; Dinah had played the best in the other two.

"The Environmental Action Club," Dinah read as they passed the next booth. "That sounds boring. I think they go around picking litter off the school lawn. Things like that."

"There's the Girls' Athletic Association." Suzanne pointed it out. "See Brady sitting there?"

"Waiting for victims," Dinah said. "Can you imagine signing up for a *gym* club?"

"No," Suzanne said. "But it looks pretty crowded over there. Isn't that Blaine What's-her-name? Standing right next to Brady?"

"She's Brady's pet. She *loves* Brady, and Brady loves her. Blaine stays after class every day and helps Brady copy everybody's points off into her great big grade book."

"Does she really?" Suzanne asked.

"No," Dinah said. "But it's the kind of thing she *would* do. Let's go over there and pretend we want to join. Just for fun."

Dinah jogged over to the GAA booth. Suzanne followed, walking. At the booth, Dinah jogged in place for a bit. "Got to stay in shape!" she said to the group assembled there.

"Do you run every day?" Blaine asked her.

"Just five miles," Dinah said modestly. "That is, on the days I don't swim or lift weights."

"You look pretty winded right now," Blaine said. "It's dumb to overdo it. You can injure yourself that way."

Glad of the excuse, Dinah stopped jogging. She was definitely *out* of shape. While she tried to catch her breath, she leaned against the GAA table and pretended to stretch her calf muscles the way she had seen real joggers do. Blaine watched her, unsmiling.

"I'm trying out for the girls' field hockey team," Blaine said. "Are you? They took the trophy at the regionals last year and went all the way to the state finals."

"I might," Dinah said. "But I'm pretty busy this fall. I mean, with running all those miles and swimming all those laps."

"And weight lifting," Blaine reminded her. Did she know that Dinah was joking? Maybe Blaine didn't think the GAA was something to joke about. Dinah wouldn't like it if other kids made fun of the Drama Club.

Feeling guilty now, Dinah straightened up from her calf-stretching and said, "Actually, Suzanne and I are joining the Drama Club, and I'm running for class president. I turned my petition in before I came here. It's time JFK had a girl for class president, don't you think?"

She wasn't sure how Blaine would respond, but

Blaine said, "I certainly do." There was something about her tone Dinah couldn't figure out.

"Blaine!" another girl called to them from behind the GAA booth. "How's this for a slogan?"

The girl held up a sign lettered with marker pens on a large sheet of manila paper. It said: ELECT A GIRL FOR A *CHANGE*. BLAINE YARBOROUGH FOR SIXTH-GRADE PRESIDENT.

"It's great, Jessica. I love it!" Blaine called back. Then she turned to Dinah and held out her hand. "May the better girl win," she said.

Dinah shook hands, meeting Blaine's cool, level gaze.

"May the better girl win," she echoed.

But down deep Dinah didn't want the better girl to win. She wanted *Dinah* to win. And something told her it was going to be even harder to beat cool, perfect Blaine Yarborough than to beat grinning, know-it-all Jason Winfield.

Four

Dinah sprang out of bed Saturday morning, ready to spend the whole day making campaign posters—great big ones, huge enormous ones—and enough buttons for every sixth grader at JFK, all 242 of them.

"Can you drive me to the art-supplies place this morning so I can get some poster board and some really, really bright marker pens?" she asked her parents at breakfast.

"I'm sorry, honey," Dinah's mother said, "but I'm counting on you to help me today at Mrs. Briscoe's."

"I helped you last week," Dinah protested.

"And I'd like you to help me this week, too. Mrs. Briscoe is the most challenging client I've ever had, and I want to do my best by her."

"Why can't Daddy help you? I'll baby-sit for Benjamin."

As if to demonstrate her baby-sitting skills, Dinah reached down and handed Benjamin his squeaky rubber monkey rattle. From the old quilt on the floor where he lay, Benjamin gave her a toothless grin. Then he stuck the rattle in his mouth and gnawed on it. He wouldn't eat cookies, but he'd eat a squeaky rubber monkey rattle. Babies were strange.

"I'm afraid not, honey. You're not quite ready for that much responsibility. Besides, it's you I want. I think it will do Mrs. Briscoe good to have the company of someone young and lively for a change. Come on, another few weeks and we'll be done. You don't want Mrs. Briscoe to have to go to a nursing home, do you?"

Dinah shrugged. Old people went to nursing homes all the time. It wasn't the end of the world. "Why can't her dumb daughter help you? I mean, it's her mother."

Dinah's mother began clearing the cereal bowls from the table. "Because she's hired *me* to do the job, and I need help from *my* daughter."

Dinah looked at her mother. "If it was Grammy, you wouldn't pay somebody else to fix her house up. You'd do it yourself."

"And if everybody felt that way, I'd be out of a job, wouldn't I?" was all her mother said. "Go run and get dressed, and we'll leave here by nine."

"Why can't *Benjamin* help you? He's young and lively."

"Dinah," her father said, "if I wanted somebody to drive me to the art-supplies store this afternoon and buy me some poster board and marker pens, I'd be a little more cooperative this morning."

"Oh," Dinah said. "Well, if you put it that way."

She swooped down on Benjamin and gave him a big, slobbery kiss. "Just you wait," she told him. "Some wonderful jobs are going to come your way in another eleven years or so, you lucky bambino."

When Dinah walked into Mrs. Briscoe's house half an hour later, she was impressed with how much progress her mother had made in a week. Mrs. Briscoe's kitchen now looked like a normal person's kitchen. The pantry shelves were neatly arranged, so that cans of tomatoes stood next to cans of tomatoes, cans of soup next to cans of soup. And the butternut squash was nowhere to be seen.

Dinah sort of missed it. But she knew how hard her mother had worked, so all she said was, "I can't believe it, Mom. It's so *organized*."

"And look, Dinah," Mrs. Briscoe said merrily. She pointed to the shelf above the stove. "The frog teapot! So you must have tea with me today. I insist. Unless—" She turned to Dinah's mother. "Is Dinah allowed to drink tea? We can brew it weak, with lots of lemon—if I can find the lemons. . . ."

"They're in the crisper," Dinah's mother said. "I'm afraid I can't join you. I have to make some progress on the living room today. But Dinah would love some tea, I know she would. Right, Dinah?"

Wrong. Dinah had had tea a couple of times in her life, and she hadn't particularly liked it. And she didn't want to be left alone with somebody as old as Mrs.

Briscoe. Dinah wasn't used to old people. Her grandparents on both sides were young, for grandparents. Mrs. Briscoe was old enough to be Dinah's great-grandmother. She was *ancient*, and her hands were veiny, and her chin trembled sometimes when she talked.

"Don't you need help?" Dinah asked her mother hopefully. She could be young and lively company for Mrs. Briscoe some other day.

"Oh, don't worry, honey," her mother said. "I can manage fine alone."

"We can make it a party," Mrs. Briscoe said. "I haven't had a party since Ruthie lived here, and that's been—oh, it's been thirty years now. We'll have—I know!—we'll have buttered toast! Cut into little triangles. Won't that be lovely?"

"I'll leave you two, then," Dinah's mother said.

Dinah glared at her, but she turned her head so that Mrs. Briscoe wouldn't see.

Mrs. Briscoe put the kettle on to boil. "There's my friend the black squirrel," she said, pointing out the window. "He lost his tail in a quarrel last spring, poor fellow, but he's learned to balance remarkably well without it. I watch for him every day from this window. What old people would do without windows, I don't know."

"There're no windows in my new school," Dinah said, as if the absence of windows were somehow Mrs. Briscoe's fault.

"No windows!" Mrs. Briscoe cried. "But that's terrible. How do you see outside? How can you know if the wind is blowing or the snow is falling?"

"You can't," Dinah said. "I hate it."

"Of course you do! I would, too."

The little old lady's warm expression of indignant sympathy made Dinah feel a bit better about the tea party. Mrs. Briscoe poured the tea from the mouth of the frog teapot and offered Dinah sugar and a fat slice of lemon. Dinah took a small sip from her china teacup. The tea was sweet and lemony, nicer than the tea she remembered.

"In my old school, I climbed out the window once, onto the roof," Dinah told Mrs. Briscoe, making conversation.

"Did you, really?" Mrs. Briscoe sounded impressed rather than shocked.

"It was raining, and I felt like— There's this movie called *Singin' in the Rain*. In it a man named Gene Kelly does this dance in the rain where he gets completely sopping wet stomping in all the puddles, but he doesn't care because he's so happy. That's what I felt like doing."

"And you did."

"But then Artie Adams closed the window so I couldn't get back in and the substitute teacher caught me and I had to go to see the principal."

"He must have been rather cross with you."

"I guess so." Dinah took another long sip of tea. "But it was worth it."

Mrs. Briscoe nodded. " '. . . for a breath of ecstasy / Give all you have been, or could be.' "

Dinah stared. How could someone like Mrs. Briscoe know just how she felt?

"That's a line from a poem I've always loved: 'Barter,' by Sara Teasdale. Would you care for some buttered toast?"

Dinah took three slices.

"What's the view like from your bedroom window at home?" Mrs. Briscoe asked her then.

Dinah liked the question. It was certainly more interesting than "How old are you?" or "What's your favorite subject in school?"

"It's nice," Dinah said. "I can see the Harmons' house next door, and sometimes they have their curtains open and I can see Mr. Harmon in the kitchen frying pancakes. And beyond that there're some trees, and in the summer that's all I can see, but in the winter the leaves fall off, and I can see a little bit of the mountains."

"Pancakes, trees, and mountains. Yes, I would say that *is* a nice view," Mrs. Briscoe said.

When the last wedge of buttered toast was gone, Mrs. Briscoe led Dinah to what had been the dining room, but now served as a bedroom. Setting up a ground-floor bedroom had been one of Dinah's mother's main objectives in organizing Mrs. Briscoe, because it was so difficult for her to climb stairs.

"I promised to show you my frog collection," Mrs.

45

Briscoe said. She opened the glass door of a corner cabinet, and Dinah knelt down to see.

"Oh!" Dinah exclaimed.

There were dozens of frogs made of every conceivable material—porcelain, clay, wood, stone, fabric, straw. One was as tiny as Dinah's thumbnail; others were life-size or larger.

"Go ahead and touch them if you'd like," Mrs. Briscoe said. "They're sociable frogs. They've missed having company as much as I have."

Dinah took a plump porcelain frog out of the case. He was dressed elegantly, in breeches, vest, and embroidered waistcoat.

"Actually," Mrs. Briscoe said, "my collection includes toads, as well as frogs. This is Toad of Toad Hall, the greatest toad of all."

"Who's he?" Dinah had to ask.

"You don't know *The Wind in the Willows*? It was my favorite of all books as a child."

Dinah shook her head.

"But you *must*! When your dear mother turns to organizing my books, I'll ask her to look for it, and I'll give you my copy. It's hardly any use to me these days, I'm afraid, with my vision so poor. I don't suppose that—if you wouldn't mind, that is—you could read bits and snatches of it aloud to me, over more tea and toast."

Dinah hesitated. The tea party had turned out to be sort of fun, after all, but she didn't want to make a *habit* of sitting around talking to old people. Her mother had said they'd be done in another couple of weeks. Could they read a whole book by then? And first they had to find it.

"Of course, I know how busy you young people are these days. . . ." Mrs. Briscoe's voice trailed off uncertainly.

Dinah didn't know what to say. She *was* busy. She had a presidential campaign to run against two tough opponents. As soon as it was over, the Drama Club was going to hold auditions for the fall play, which wasn't going to be *Hamlet*, Dinah had found out, but *You're a Good Man, Charlie Brown*. So Dinah might be Lucy, or maybe Peppermint Patty, or even Snoopy, if they'd let a girl be Snoopy. Besides, middle school teachers gave a lot of homework, every night. Putting her mark on middle school was going to be a full-time job.

"I have to go ask," Dinah said. "In case my mother needs me to help her some more."

I need you! Dinah willed her mother to say. But her mother looked up with a smile from the ocean of newspapers that surrounded her.

"That *would* be helping, more than anything, Dinah. Mrs. Briscoe's biggest problem isn't clutter, you know, it's loneliness."

"How many pages are in *The Wind in the Willows?*" Dinah asked.

"Oh, I don't know, honey. I don't think it matters. I think that was just Mrs. Briscoe's way of saying that she'd like for you to visit again. You can consider it your contribution to Seabrooke Organizing, Incorporated."

Slowly Dinah walked back to the dining room. Organizing Mrs. Briscoe was turning out to be a lot of work for her mother's junior partner. And at the end of it, what would she have to show for all her time? She would have read some moldy old book about a moldy old toad. It was hard not to see it as a waste of effort and energy that could have been better spent on a dazzling election campaign.

Mrs. Briscoe looked up at her expectantly.

"She said I can," Dinah told her. She realized that she was still holding Toad of Toad Hall. Gently, she set him back in the cabinet.

Mrs. Briscoe's face crinkled into a smile. Dinah made herself smile back at her.

"I'll come see you often," Dinah promised brightly. "I mean, as often as I can." *I mean, as often as I have to.*

Five

Dinah took the cap off a bright purple felt-tipped pen. She tested the color on a scrap of paper. It was bright, all right. Then she began lettering her first poster. DINAH SEABROOKE FOR SIXTH-GRADE PRESIDENT! she wrote on the large square of poster board. SHE'S DYNAMITE! Underneath she drew a stick of dynamite about to explode.

"Can you tell this is supposed to be a stick of dynamite?" she asked Suzanne. They were at Dinah's house, on Sunday afternoon, working at the dining room table.

Suzanne studied Dinah's poster. "No," she said. "It looks like an empty roll of toilet paper."

Dinah drew a wick at the end of it.

"Now it looks like a candle," Suzanne told her.

Dinah added some stars—red and orange and yellow—to suggest sparks.

"A firecracker," Suzanne said. "Close enough. I don't know what to put on my posters. I wrote 'Vote for Suzanne Kelly' on one, but I didn't leave enough room to say that I'm running for secretary."

"You need a slogan," Dinah said. "Like 'Dinah Seabrooke is dynamite.' Something catchy, with your name in it. So . . . Suzanne Kelly is . . ." Dinah tried to think of words that started with *s*. "Is super. How about that? Super-duper Suzanne!"

"I don't know," Suzanne said. "It seems . . . well, braggy, don't you think? To stick up signs all over the school saying how great you are?"

"You have to," Dinah said. "It's part of being in politics."

"But I'm not super, I'm really not. I mean, I think I can do the job, but I don't think I'm wonderful or anything."

"Okay," Dinah said. "How about 'Suzanne Kelly— she can do the job.' "

Suzanne's face brightened. "I like it. At least it's true."

"I don't," Dinah said. "It's true, and it's boring. Wait a minute. How about this: 'Suzanne can!' "

"Can what?"

"Can do the job. But this way it's short and snappy, and it rhymes. 'Suzanne Kelly for sixth-grade secretary. Suzanne can!' "

"You really like that better?"

"A hundred times better," Dinah said. "Let's make twenty signs each, and we'll put them up on Monday."

Suzanne picked out a few dark-brown M&M's from the one-pound bag that lay open on the table. Dark-brown M&Ms were Suzanne's favorite. "There's this boy," she said, carefully lining up the M&Ms on the edge of her poster board, "in our English class. He's in our math class, too. Greg Thomas."

"I know him," Dinah said. "He wouldn't sign my petition."

"Why not?"

"He wanted to know what my platform was. You know, what I want to achieve as president. Something like that. I said I didn't have one yet, so he didn't sign. What about him?" Dinah found herself dreading Suzanne's answer.

"Nothing. I was just wondering. I mean, do you think he's cute?"

Dinah reached for the scissors, knocking Suzanne's M&M's out of line.

"No, I don't think he's cute. I'm running *against* a boy for president. I don't think any boys are cute, especially boys who don't sign my petition."

Suzanne didn't say anything. Slowly she began coloring in the letters she had outlined lightly in pencil: SUZANNE CAN.

"Why?" Dinah asked in spite of herself. "*You* don't think he's cute, do you?"

"Kind of," Suzanne admitted, without looking up from her poster.

"I bet he didn't sign it because I'm a girl. That was the real reason, whatever he *said*."

"I don't think Greg's like that."

"I bet he votes for Jason Winfield. All the boys are

going to vote for Jason. Jason said they were, this morning in homeroom."

"*Jason* said. Jason doesn't know everything."

"Neither does Greg Thomas."

"I never said he did. I just said— Oh, forget it."

Dinah held up her finished sign. "Does *that* look like a stick of dynamite?" This time she had drawn jagged lines coming out from the end, like lightning.

"Definitely." Suzanne held up her poster. "You're sure people aren't going to read this and say, 'Can *what*?' "

"I'm sure," Dinah said. They propped the posters up on the sideboard to admire them. One down, nineteen to go.

Suzanne didn't mention Greg Thomas for the rest of the afternoon, and Dinah didn't, either. As far as Dinah was concerned, the less said about boys, the better.

As soon as Dinah walked through the front doors of JFK Middle School Monday morning she saw it, a large green poster lettered in bold blue ink: JASON WINFIELD FOR SIXTH-GRADE PRESIDENT. Jason must have raced through the doors the second they opened, his roll of masking tape in hand.

"Look." Dinah grabbed hold of Suzanne. "I'm going to put up *two*, one on either side of his. You'd better start sticking yours up, too."

"Are we allowed to put signs up anywhere we want?" Suzanne asked.

"Nobody said not to."

With only ten minutes till the tardy bell, Dinah worked fast. She taped up poster after poster, twenty feet apart, down the entire length of the first-floor hallway. DINAH FOR PRESIDENT! DINAH FOR PRESIDENT! DINAH FOR PRESIDENT! Everywhere she turned she saw her name in great big letters. This was the way a middle school should look.

During English class, Dinah lettered construction-paper campaign buttons behind the propped-up pages of *Fun with Grammar*.

"Denise," Mr. Prensky called out, "I don't know what you're working on, but I suspect it isn't direct and indirect objects."

Dinah held her breath. Last week Mr. Prensky had made another girl "share her work" with the rest of the class. Her "work" had turned out to be a drippy love poem to the boy who sat behind her.

"Why don't you share your work with the rest of the class?"

Dinah gathered up her buttons.

"Denise? We're all waiting."

Dinah walked to the front of the room. "I'm making campaign buttons," she said. "This one says 'Dinah Seabrooke for sixth-grade president.' This one says 'Vote for Dinah, she's dynamite.' And this one says 'Dynamite Dinah.' I think I have enough for everybody. Do you want me to pass them out or just stick one or two up here on the bulletin board?"

"That won't be necessary, Dinah," Mr. Prensky

said coldly. "Put them away, or I'll take them away, and you can spend the rest of our grammar lesson making campaign buttons in Mr. Roemer's office."

Dinah went back to her seat. Poor Mr. Prensky. How could he have known that by making Dinah share her work he'd give her class time for a free political advertisement?

"The rest of us are on page twenty-five, Dinah," Mr. Prensky told her then.

He'd learned her name, too.

Dinah pinned a campaign button to her gym clothes as she changed for second-period gym. She was curious to see how many points Brady would take off for it. Maybe next year Brady would include "campaign button on gym wear" in the official penalty list, and Dinah would have made another mark, however small, on JFK Middle School.

The class lined up for the roll call. Miss Brady walked along the line, eyeing each girl in turn. Dinah felt her button glowing like a red traffic light.

"Curly Top. Get that button off your shirt." Miss Brady made a notation in her roll book.

Dinah unpinned the button and slipped it into her shorts pocket. "Um, Miss Brady?"

"Yes?"

"I was just wondering. I mean, does a campaign button count like 'dirty gym wear, ten points'? Or 'sneakers without laces, five points'? "

"I don't like that tone, Curly Top," Miss Brady

said. "Any more lip, and you'll have earned yourself a zero for the day."

Dinah didn't like Miss Brady's tone, either, but she didn't make any more witty comments. She had to admit it: She was afraid of Miss Brady. Or not afraid, exactly. But if she had a choice between getting into trouble with Brady and not getting into trouble with Brady, she'd just as soon not.

All morning long, between classes, Dinah taped up campaign posters frantically. She saw lots of posters for Jason, fewer for Blaine. But each of Blaine's posters was beautifully lettered, almost like calligraphy, and brilliantly positioned for maximum exposure: outside the cafeteria, next to the library, by the mirror in the second-floor girls' room. Dinah kept an eye out for Suzanne's competition, too. As far as she could tell, three other girls were running for class secretary, all of them named Katie: Katie Richards, Katie Steinhart, and Katie Wong. So Suzanne had a big advantage in not being Katie the Fourth.

At lunch Dinah gulped down half a sandwich. Then she stationed herself by the conveyor belt. As kids carried out their dirty trays, she handed them campaign buttons and gave a big beaming smile. "I'm Dynamite Dinah. I'm running for sixth-grade president. Vote for me!" Did real, grown-up presidential candidates say "Vote for me"? Probably not. They got their supporters to say things like that for them. Dinah could ask Suzanne to stand by the conveyor belt, saying "Vote for Dinah!" and Dinah could stand next to her, saying "Vote for Suzanne!" They could have a little rally, where they each took turns cheering for the other.

No. One friend did not a rally make. Better to stand alone by the trash can, chirping "Vote for me!"

Sixth-period social studies was the only class, besides homeroom, that Dinah shared with both Jason and Blaine. As soon as the bell rang and the class had settled down, Mr. Dixon picked up his seating chart. "Seabrooke! Winfield! Yarborough! I believe you three are all running for class president."

Dinah nodded, as did the others.

"Class, I hope you feel suitably honored. With only three declared candidates so far, the next president of the sixth grade is likely in our midst."

Mr. Dixon picked up the long pointer that he kept on his desk. He gave a loud whack to the calendar on the wall behind him.

"Two weeks from Wednesday—October second—we'll have a debate. A *presidential* debate. The rest of you, come with questions for our illustrious candidates. Tough questions. No holds barred. And you three, come with some answers. Answers, not slogans."

He gave the calendar a second whack. "Kids!" Another whack. "Posterity is watching you! And now posterity is going to watch you take a pop quiz on last week's current events. Clear your desks!"

Posterity is watching you. Dinah liked the thought,

even though she knew Dixon was half-sarcastic in saying it. Dinah was determined to give posterity a debate worth watching.

"We need to make more posters," she told Suzanne on the bus ride home.

"I still have a few of mine left."

"Suzanne! A lot of good posters do when they're in your *locker*! The Katies have tons of posters up. You should, too. Blaine even has posters in the girls' room. Do you think Jason has posters in the boys' room?" Dinah had a daring thought. "I could dash in there tomorrow morning, just for a minute, and stick up some of ours."

"You wouldn't! Get one of the boys to do it for you."

"Like who?" Dinah jeered.

"Greg would do it."

Dinah made a face.

"He's nice, Dinah, he really is. I think he— Well, he doesn't *like* me, exactly. But he sort of does. He asked me for one of my buttons."

"Well, he didn't ask me for one of mine. Okay, forget the boys' room. But we're making more posters this afternoon. And tomorrow we're putting up every single one. I'm going to put one on the front door of the school. So that everyone can see it while they're waiting outside for the bell to ring."

"I want mine *inside*," Suzanne said quickly.

"Or what if I made a big banner and taped it across the Welcome, Students sign on the school lawn! I mean, it's the third week of school now. We're about as welcomed as we're going to be."

Suzanne didn't answer. Then, just before their bus stop, she asked, "Do you think it *means* anything if a boy asks for one of your campaign buttons?"

"It means he wants to marry you," Dinah said solemnly, "and have ten children, five boys and five girls."

"Oh, Dinah," Suzanne said. But she blushed as she said it.

The next morning Dinah's father drove the girls to school early so that Dinah could tape up her banner and front-door sign before the first bus load of students arrived. The banner was so big that cars driving past JFK Middle School would be able to read it without slowing down: DYNAMITE DINAH FOR SIXTH-GRADE PRESIDENT. It sent shivers up Dinah's spine when she looked at it from the sidewalk. Jason and Blaine would have a fit when they saw it.

Sure enough: "We're not allowed to put signs up *outside*," Blaine told Dinah across the aisle in homeroom. She kept the same patient tone she always used in explaining things to Dinah.

"Says who?"

"Roemer's going to make you take it down," Jason said.

"You just wish you'd thought of it first," Dinah shot back.

Over the PA system some girl led the Pledge of Allegiance. Then Mr. Roemer cleared his throat.

"Good morning. Today the boys' soccer team takes on the Wilmington Wildcats at four o'clock, away. Good luck, boys! The girls' field hockey team takes on Lakeside, here at home. I hope you'll all turn out to cheer for the ladies."

Blaine glowed, as if the principal had instructed everyone to cheer for her personally.

Then: "Last call. Petitions for class office are due on my desk today by 3:18. I want to make it clear that *all* campaign posters are to be displayed *inside* the school. Any posters or banners displayed on the doors of the school or on the outdoor announcement board will be promptly removed and discarded. Thank you for your cooperation in keeping our school grounds neat."

"See?" Blaine asked, when Roemer had finished the announcements.

"Nice try, Seabrooke," Jason taunted.

Dinah barely heard them. She could hardly wait to tell her parents, Benjamin, the Kellys—the world. It was only the third week of school and already her dream from the first day had come true. She, Dinah Seabrooke, lowly sixth grader, the smallest of frogs, had been the secret star of morning announcements.

Six

After school that day, Dinah met her mother at Mrs. Briscoe's house to help out for a couple of hours before dinner. As her mother bundled up old newspapers in the living room, Dinah gave her the top headlines from all the exciting election news. Then she made herself join Mrs. Briscoe in the kitchen.

"I'm just brewing our tea," Mrs. Briscoe said, greeting her. The frog teapot sat on the kitchen table, wide-eyed, as if he had been waiting all day for Dinah to arrive. Next to him lay a faded, well-worn book: *The Wind in the Willows*.

"You found it," Dinah said, pointing.

"Your mother found it, marvel that she is. I thought if you didn't mind, we could start reading this afternoon."

Mind? The sooner they started, the sooner they'd finish. "I don't mind," Dinah said. She gobbled down two wedges of toast, gulped half a cup of tea, and opened the book to Chapter One.

" 'The Mole had been working very hard all the morning, spring cleaning his little home. . . .' "

Dinah had planned to read fast, but there were a lot of hard words in the book, and the sentences and paragraphs were so long that they forced her to go slowly. As she read, Dinah found herself becoming absorbed in the story, caught up in the beauty of the language and the feelings it captured. When she finally reached the end of the first chapter, she sighed with pleasure.

Across the table from her, Mrs. Briscoe sat with her eyes closed, but Dinah could tell that she wasn't asleep, that Mrs. Briscoe, too, had been transported to the world of Mole and Rat's riverbank.

"I don't know what all the words mean," Dinah said. "I probably read some of them wrong."

"You read splendidly," Mrs. Briscoe told her, opening her eyes to pour Dinah some more tea. "You could have a career on the stage."

That was what Dinah had often thought herself. But it was nice to have someone else say it for her.

"Is there time to read another chapter?" Dinah asked.

"I think so," Mrs. Briscoe said. She lowered her voice, as if sharing a delightful secret: "The next chapter is where we make the acquaintance of Mr. Toad."

Dinah wiped buttery crumbs from her fingers and began. "Chapter Two: The Open Road."

Chapter Two was even better than Chapter One,

because Toad was such a wonderful character to read about—boastful and conceited, driven by passionate whims and wild enthusiasms.

"So what do you think of my friend Toad?" Mrs. Briscoe asked when Dinah had finished. It was growing dark outside now, and Dinah's mother appeared in the kitchen doorway, signaling her that it was time to go.

"He's my favorite," Dinah said. "I like how he gets an idea into his head and then wants to do *that* more than anything in the world. And how he brags about himself. I mean, he *shouldn't*, but it's funny when he does. I used to know someone sort of like him."

Dinah meant that she used to *be* someone sort of like him, when she was younger, back in fifth grade. It was odd to come across a character in a book who was so in love with himself, and have him come right out and *say* it.

"Dinah, honey, Benjamin will be wondering where we are," Dinah's mother told her, and smiled apologetically at Mrs. Briscoe.

"I have to go," Dinah said, puzzled that the hours could have flown so swiftly.

"Till next time, then," Mrs. Briscoe said. "Dinah, thank you."

"So it wasn't so bad, was it?" Dinah's mother asked her in the car on the way home.

"I didn't say that," Dinah said. She had to admit that *The Wind in the Willows* was a wonderful book. But she didn't have to admit it out loud, to her mother.

On Saturday the whole Seabrooke family gathered at Mrs. Briscoe's house to load half a century's newspapers and empty glasses and jars into the minivan Dinah's father had borrowed for the occasion. There would be no time for reading that day; except for useless Benjamin, everyone would have to work, and work hard, to get the job done.

"We'll have to make at least two trips to the recycling center," Dinah's father said as he surveyed the several hundred brown grocery bags stuffed full of newsprint.

"At least she saved bags as well as papers," Dinah's mother said. "She was right to think they'd come in handy sometime."

As her parents began carrying the bags out to the van, Dinah took Benjamin inside to meet Mrs. Briscoe.

"Why, you're so fat!" Mrs. Briscoe told Benjamin, clapping her hands with delight. "You're as fat as butter!"

Dinah had noticed that babies were often given odd compliments. No grown-up would like to be told he was as fat as butter. But Benjamin was definitely plump. He had three wobbly chins, and dimples instead of knuckles. Now he reached for Mrs. Briscoe's glasses.

"Don't give them to him," Dinah advised. "He'll just put them in his mouth and try to eat them."

"Would he like some buttered toast?" Mrs. Briscoe asked.

"No," Dinah said. "He doesn't like food."

"Doesn't like food! You could have fooled me, Master Benjamin, you chubby darling thing, you!"

"He likes milk. Well, formula, actually. Sometimes he'll let you give him a spoonful of rice cereal, if it's really thin and there're no lumps in it."

"And I don't have either one to offer him." Mrs. Briscoe sounded disappointed. "But I do have some applesauce. Do you think he'd try a nice spoonful of applesauce?"

Dinah remembered that her mother had been planning to buy some baby applesauce for Benjamin that weekend. "He might."

In the kitchen, Dinah held Benjamin on her lap while Mrs. Briscoe spooned a small amount of applesauce into a Pyrex cup.

"I even have a baby spoon, I think, if your dear mother didn't—no, here it is! All right, Benjamin, open wide!"

Benjamin clamped his mouth shut.

With her free hand, Mrs. Briscoe stroked him gently under the chin. Surprised, Benjamin opened his mouth, and she inserted the tip of the baby spoon, with the tiniest bit of applesauce on it.

Benjamin tasted it. He swallowed. He screwed up his face into a pucker. Then he opened his mouth for more.

"He likes it!" Dinah was amazed. Benjamin ate a second spoonful, and a third. He looked like a baby bird in the nest, obediently opening his little beak for bites of a juicy worm.

When he had finished the entire cup, Dinah ran outside to tell her parents. "You can put the sticker on his baby calendar!" she announced. "He ate a whole bowlful of solid food."

Dinah's mother hurried inside to verify this miracle for herself. Dinah stayed to help her father.

"Can you handle one of those newspaper bags?" he asked her. "They're pretty heavy."

Dinah lifted one to see. She managed to lug it down Mrs. Briscoe's front steps, then gratefully let her father take it from her.

"Hey, could you guys use some help?" The voice was familiar. Dinah turned to see Greg Thomas standing on the front porch next door, watching them, no doubt thinking he was something wonderful just because he was a boy.

"No," Dinah flung back. She'd carry a hundred newspaper bags weighing a hundred pounds apiece before she'd accept help from the enemy.

But her father called to Greg, "We sure could. Want to lend a hand?"

Traitor! But what could Dinah expect? Her father was a former boy himself.

The work did go faster with Greg helping. He was small but wiry, and Dinah could tell from the apparent ease with which he hoisted the bags that he was strong. Leaving Mrs. Briscoe to watch Benjamin, Dinah's mother rejoined the others. They formed themselves into a sort of newspaper brigade. Greg lifted a bag of papers, gave it to Dinah, who gave it to her mother, who handed it off to Dinah's father. Soon the van was filled.

"Thanks a bunch . . ." Dinah's father turned to Greg, waiting for him to supply the name.

"Greg. Dinah and I have some classes together at school."

"It's always nice to meet one of Dinah's friends," Dinah's mother said.

Dinah didn't say anything. Greg wasn't exactly her *friend*. Boys weren't friends. In fact, it was closer to the truth to say that Greg was trying to steal Dinah's best friend away.

Dinah's father climbed up into the van for the first trip to the recycling center. Dinah's mother went inside to begin preparing the next load. Dinah turned to walk away.

"Hey, are you mad at me about something?" Greg asked. " 'Cause I didn't sign your petition? I didn't sign Winfield's petition, either. I just think that if someone runs for class president, she should be prepared to tell people something about her plans for the office. That's all."

Dinah had a sudden hunch. "You signed Blaine's."

"Yeah."

"What's *her* platform?"

"School spirit. She thinks kids today are too apathetic. You know, that they don't care enough about school activities. So she wants to try to get everyone involved in a club or sport or something."

"Whoop-de-doo," Dinah said.

"At least she *has* a platform," Greg said mildly. "See you Monday."

He walked off, whistling. What was *wrong* with her, Dinah wondered, that she wanted to pick up the last bag of papers and hurl it after him as he went?

Dinah rode in the van with her father on his next trip to the recycling center.

"Wait till you see this place," he told her. "Mrs. Briscoe's papers hardly fill half of one of their bins. It's incredible how much newspaper there is in the world. And if it weren't for recycling centers like this one, it'd all go straight into a landfill."

"What's a landfill?" Dinah asked.

"A dump. A garbage dump. At the rate we're going, the whole planet is going to be one."

Dinah was surprised at her father's tone of voice. She didn't know he felt so strongly about recycling. Her parents always bundled up newspapers for the once-a-week pickup and separated glass containers and aluminum cans from the rest of their trash. But they just did it; they didn't make a big *thing* out of it.

At the center, two young men helped Mr. Seabrooke unload Mrs. Briscoe's bottles and jars into an enormous bin. Feeling in the way, Dinah walked over to stare at the long row of newspaper bins. Her father was right. There were a lot of newspapers in the world. It would be pretty disgusting if they were all just thrown away.

"Do you know how much solid waste the United States creates every day?" one of the recycling guys asked Dinah, coming up behind her. "Four hundred and fifty thousand tons."

What could Dinah say? "Wow."

"Do you know how many pounds of paper the average person throws away every year? Newspaper, magazines, office paper, *junk mail*? Four hundred eighty-one pounds."

Dinah herself liked junk mail, if it came addressed to her. One of her favorite letters had come a week before. It said: "DINAH SEABROOKE, A MILLION DOLLAR SWEEPSTAKES PRIZE IS WAITING IN YOUR NAME! YES, DINAH SEABROOKE, $1,000,000 CAN BE YOURS TODAY!" That letter wasn't going to any landfill. Dinah had it tacked up on the bulletin board next to her bed. But most junk mail was sent to people other than Dinah, people like her parents, who threw away sweepstakes entries without even opening them.

"Wow," Dinah said again.

"Do you know how many trees would be saved if one entire edition of the Sunday *New York Times* was recycled?"

As a matter of fact, Dinah didn't.

"Seventy-five thousand. Or look at schools. There's incredible waste in schools. Your school, if it's like about every other school in America, throws away literally tons of paper every year."

"Wow," Dinah repeated automatically, but she felt an idea, like a great big dinosaur egg, struggling to hatch.

"Teachers crank out those Dittos, kids fill them out, hand them in, get their grades, throw them away. Spelling tests, math work sheets, 'What I Did on My Summer Vacation'—it all goes straight to the land-fill."

"Why?" Dinah asked. "Couldn't they recycle stuff like that?"

"Sure, they *could*. But they don't. Not one school in the county has a recycling program in place. Too much trouble. Too much hassle. I mean, it's just a matter of saving the planet. Why put yourself out for *that*?"

"So if a school wanted to start a recycling program, you'd take the stuff? You'd have a bin just for Dittos?"

"For mixed paper. We already do." He jerked a thumb in its direction.

Dinah wanted to make sure she had this straight. "So if someone started a recycling program, like at JFK Middle School, they could bring the stuff here? Like if a class president or somebody got one started?"

"You bet. You got anyone in mind?"

"Me," Dinah said.

She had her platform.

Seven

"Greg is in the Environmental Action Club," Suzanne said at their campaign strategy session Monday afternoon at Dinah's house. "He could probably get you some information about recycling to use on your new posters."

Dinah ignored the suggestion. "So some of the posters will say 'Save the planet. Vote for Dinah Seabrooke. Vote for Recycling.' And some will say 'Down on dumps? Up with Seabrooke and recycling.' Can you think of any other good slogans?"

" 'Trash, no! Dinah, yes!' "

"Suzanne! That really *is* good. I'll put that on my buttons. My parents have given me some extra allowance for helping out at Mrs. Briscoe's, but I've borrowed ahead on it till Thanksgiving to buy all these new supplies. I wish I'd had my platform before I made the first batch of signs."

Suzanne didn't say anything, but Dinah knew what she was thinking: *You should have listened to Greg.*

"But I wanted the *right* platform," Dinah said. "Not something dumb like Blaine's." Dinah switched to a high mocking voice. " 'Get involved. Vote for Blaine.' 'Show your spirit. Blaine Yarborough for sixth-grade president.' Jason has a platform, too, something about sports. The signs I saw today said 'More for sports. Vote Winfield' and 'Join the Winfield campaign. Make JFK a school of champions.' "

"I'm glad I'm running for secretary," Suzanne said. "It's a lot easier."

"You're going to win," Dinah said. "It's too hard to tell the Katies apart."

"That's what Greg says."

Dinah shot Suzanne a warning look. "Do you want to help me make signs, or do you want to talk about Greg Thomas?" she demanded.

"Both." Suzanne giggled.

Dinah groaned.

"Speaking of boys," Suzanne went on, "the boys' soccer team plays tomorrow, at home. A lot of the girls in our class are going. Do you want to stick around for it after school?"

"Are you kidding?"

"It would be a great place to hand out campaign buttons," Suzanne pointed out.

Dinah had a sudden vision of herself climbing ever higher through the bleachers as the sports fans mobbed her for a handshake or an autograph. During halftime she could give a rousing campaign speech that would have the crowds cheering so loudly that they'd drown out the beginning of the second half of the game.

"Okay," Dinah said. "I'll go." Then she remembered. "No. I can't. I have to help my mother at Mrs. Briscoe's stupid house." The pleasures of reading *The Wind in the Willows* paled beside the splendid scene Dinah had imagined.

Suzanne looked disappointed, but she didn't protest.

"My mom'll be done over there in another week or so," Dinah said, "and then I'll never have to visit Mrs. Briscoe again, and I can go to all the games I want."

By then the campaign would be over, too, but Dinah could attend the soccer games as President Dinah, inspiring JFK's team to win dazzling victories in the name of their great leader.

Would Mrs. Briscoe miss her visits, once her house was all neat and clean and organized? Dinah didn't know. But she couldn't spend her triumphant presidential year having tea and toast day after day with an eighty-year-old lady. That much would be obvious to anybody.

At Mrs. Briscoe's the next day, Dinah read as fast as she could, but she finished only two more chapters. Four down, eight to go.

"I'll come again tomorrow," she promised. She had to finish the book before her last visit.

On Wednesday, Dinah barely touched her toast before launching into Chapter Five. But Chapter Five was more than she had bargained for. Trudging with Rat in the snow, Mole catches a whiff of his old, shabby, dingy, dusty little hole, and feels it calling to him, and his whole heart yearns to return home again. As she read, silent tears began to slide down Dinah's face. When she reached the end of the chapter, she saw that Mrs. Briscoe's cheeks were wet, as well.

"I don't know how many times I've read that chapter," Mrs. Briscoe said, "but I still can't hear you read it without getting tears in my eyes."

"I went away to camp last summer," Dinah said, "and I wasn't homesick at all until the last night, when I started thinking about how my parents and Benjamin were going to come to get me the very next day, and then—well, I sort of cried. But I stuffed my pillow in my mouth so no one else would hear."

"Homesick," Mrs. Briscoe repeated. "When we're away from work we don't get worksick, or schoolsick when we're away from school. Just homesick, if we have to leave our homes."

The thought struck Dinah: Old people in nursing "homes" were *homesick*, that's what they were. They missed their homes, the familiar smell of the paint and the floorboards, the way the sunlight came through a certain window at a certain time of day and danced on a certain corner of the carpet.

"You really want to stay here, don't you?" Dinah asked Mrs. Briscoe then. "I mean, in your home."

Mrs. Briscoe nodded.

"We'll make it so you can," Dinah said confidently. "By the time we're done you'll be so organized that you can stay here till you're a hundred and ten."

"I have to admit it's more pleasant living without all that clutter," Mrs. Briscoe said, "though I can't help feeling that someone would have found a use for those newspapers someday."

"Someone did," Dinah said. "They're being recycled, so that new paper can be made out of them without cutting down any more trees. Your newspapers alone probably saved a whole forest. Now I've made recycling into my platform, for my election campaign at school. I'm running for class president, you know."

"You are? You're an actress and a politician, too?"

"Well, I haven't won yet. But I really really want to." Dinah told Mrs. Briscoe the whole story of her campaign so far, and Mrs. Briscoe listened as if she had never heard anything more fascinating.

So when it was time to go, Dinah was only one more chapter closer to finishing *The Wind in the Willows*. But with an audience like Mrs. Briscoe, it was hard for Dinah to complain.

Dinah definitely had the best platform. There was no doubt in her mind about that. Who wouldn't want to save the planet? Saving the planet was so much more important than boosting school spirit or school sports, that Dinah could hardly believe Blaine or Jason would get a single vote once everyone knew that Dinah was the one-and-only recycling candidate.

But did everyone know that? The school halls these days were so thickly covered with campaign posters that no one candidate's posters stood out. Dinah herself barely glanced at them anymore. Mr. Roemer had announced that candidates would be able to make two-minute speeches at a special assembly the day before the election. But two minutes wasn't very long, especially when everyone else was speaking for two minutes, too.

Dinah needed to do something daring and different. How fortunate it was that the daring and different happened to be her specialty.

"You're taking our recycling bucket to school?" Dinah's father asked when he saw it standing next to Dinah's backpack Friday morning. A few months before, the city had issued a bright yellow recycling bucket to each household, for collecting glass bottles and aluminum cans. WE RECYCLE WE RECYCLE WE RECYCLE it said on one side. On the other side it said DONATED BY THE FIRST NATIONAL BANK OF RIVERDALE.

"I need it for my campaign," Dinah said.

"You're going to carry it through the hallways for publicity?"

"Sort of," Dinah said. "I think the bus is coming. Bye!" Dinah had found it was better to tell her parents things after they happened, rather than before. It saved them from worrying.

Dinah held the recycling bucket on her lap on the bus ride. It was almost two feet high and as wide around as she could reach. Suzanne grinned when she saw it, but she didn't ask any questions.

The boys did.

"Is that your lunch box, Seabrooke?" Artie Adams asked her. He was the boy from Dinah's elementary school who had shut the window on her when she'd climbed onto the school roof in the rain.

"Hey, Dinah was donated by the First National Bank of Riverdale!" another boy said. "Take her back! We don't want her!"

Dinah didn't mind teasing. In fact, she liked it.

"For your information," she said sarcastically, turning the tub so that WE RECYCLE faced outward, "this is a recycling bucket. Even my baby brother knows that. I'm taking it to school today so I can publicize the schoolwide recycling program I'm going to start once I'm elected sixth-grade president."

"Dream on," Artie told her.

"Did you know that the average school throws away tons of paper every year?" Dinah asked anyone within hearing. "It's high time we started recycling some of it."

"Why don't you stop the teachers from making us do all that work in the first place?" Artie asked. "I'd vote for you then. If your name was Jason Winfield."

"Don't you even care that the whole planet is turning into a garbage dump?" Dinah asked him. She herself hadn't cared all that much a week ago, but now Artie's indifference to her platform infuriated her.

Artie shrugged. "Recycling a bunch of Dittos isn't going to make a difference."

"Of course it is!" Dinah found herself almost shouting. "Everything makes a difference."

During homeroom, Dinah kept the yellow bucket in full view on top of her desk.

"Is that your lunch, Seabrooke?" Jason asked. Really, the boys could at least try to come up with some original insults. Blaine looked at Dinah suspiciously, but said nothing.

Mr. Prensky told Dinah to take the bucket off her desk at the start of English class.

"Where should I put it?" she asked innocently. "I don't want to block the aisles, you know, and be a fire hazard."

"Did you consider leaving it in your locker?"

"It doesn't fit. It's too big around."

Mr. Prensky blew on his glasses, then wiped them with a tissue. "In the back of the room, then. Somewhere in the back. Out of view," he added.

Dinah proceeded to the rear of the room, holding the bucket so that WE RECYCLE WE RECYCLE WE RECYCLE was visible to all. Free political advertisements during first period were becoming a regular occurrence.

The recycling tub attracted its share of attention in math and science classes, too. (Dinah hid it in a corner of the locker room during gym.) At last it was time for lunch. Dinah carried the tub into the girls' room to prepare for her grand entrance into the school cafeteria. Then, a few minutes into the lunch period, she presented herself majestically in the cafeteria doorway.

She was wearing the tub on her head. It was held in place with a sash threaded through the drainage holes at its base and tied in a big floppy bow under Dinah's chin. Still, it wobbled a bit as Dinah took a small step forward. She felt like a peasant woman walking to market with an enormous bird cage balanced on her turban.

"Hey, Dinah!" Artie called to her as silence fell like a curtain of darkness on each table in turn. "What's wrong with your head?"

Laughter.

"Nothing," Dinah replied. "What's wrong is that our school has no recycling program, none at all."

"Bucket Head!" Jason yelled. "Bucket Head for president!"

Dinah refused to let herself be distracted. "Did you know that this school throws away *tons* of paper in a year? I say that's disgraceful. I say something should be done about it." Two cafeteria monitors were closing in on her, one approaching from the left, one from the right. "And something will be done about it if you vote for me on October fourth. Dinah Seabrooke for sixth-grade president!"

A few kids clapped and cheered, but Jason's supporters drowned them out with a chorus of boos.

"That's enough, Dinah," one monitor said, taking Dinah's arm. "Settle down, boys and girls. The next one of you I have to speak to can go to the office with Dinah here."

"Down with dumps!" Dinah called back over her shoulder. "Up with—" But she never got to finish.

"You. Take that thing off your head," the taller of the two monitors barked at her.

Dinah untied the sash and lifted the tub off her flattened curls.

"Why anyone would want to make herself look so ridiculous, I'm sure I don't know."

The woman didn't seem to expect an answer, but Dinah offered one, anyway. "I was trying to *say* something," she said. "I wanted to give them all a message."

"You want to send a message, call Western Union," the woman said, evidently pleased at her own wit. "Now, off to Mr. Roemer's office, and no shilly-shallying on the way."

Dinah headed down the long hallway, carrying the tub under her arm like an oversized tom-tom. She'd be just as glad when it was back in the garage again, filled with empty applesauce jars.

Everyone now knew she was the recycling candidate. That mission was accomplished. But would they cast their votes for someone nicknamed Bucket Head?

Eight

Dinah knew all about being sent to the elementary-school principal's office, but this was her first visit to a principal in middle school. She didn't even know what Mr. Roemer looked like. He was just a voice that cleared its throat and read a list of morning announcements.

Dinah waited in the outer office until one of the school secretaries looked up from her keyboard.

"The cafeteria lady sent me here because I wore this on my head." Dinah pointed to the yellow recycling bucket.

"You wore *that* on your head?"

"Nobody ever said not to," Dinah said. "I didn't know there was a rule in this school about wearing things on your head."

"Of course there is," the woman said. "The school dress code specifies that a student's clothing shall not be such as to distract other students from their studies."

Was a yellow recycling bucket *clothing*? Did lunch

count as *studies*? Dinah didn't have a chance to ask because Mr. Roemer stuck his head out of his office.

"Is there someone here to see me?" he asked. His glance fell on Dinah. "Come on in."

Dinah sat in the roomy armchair facing the principal's desk and watched him curiously. He looked very different from what Dinah had expected. The voice that came over the PA system was big and booming; Mr. Roemer himself was small and slight in build. The twitch of his neatly clipped gray mustache reminded her of somebody—the White Rabbit in *Alice in Wonderland*.

"Tell me why you're here," Mr. Roemer said in the voice that didn't match his body.

Dinah told her story. For good measure, she put in everything she could think of about the importance of a school recycling program. It wasn't every day that a student had the ear of a school principal, though this happened to Dinah more often than to many people.

"I like your platform," Mr. Roemer said when she had finished. "I wonder, though, whether creating a disturbance in the cafeteria is the best way to gain respectful attention for your ideas."

Attention, yes. But respectful? Dinah couldn't, in all truthfulness, describe the reaction of the cafeteria crowd to her unusual headgear as respectful.

"The disciplinary action I usually take in the case of a cafeteria disturbance is a week of office detention," Mr. Roemer said.

Dinah caught her breath. In elementary school, detention had practically been Dinah's middle name, but now she couldn't afford a whole week of lost afternoons. She would miss Drama Club. She would miss poster-making sessions with Suzanne. She'd even miss reading *The Wind in the Willows* with Mrs. Briscoe. To her surprise, Dinah blinked back a sudden surge of tears.

"But because of the unusual circumstances in your case," Mr. Roemer continued, "the fact that this was part of your election campaign—however misguided, I must add—I'll let you go this time with a warning." He scribbled out a pass back to lunch.

"Thank you," Dinah said. She picked up her yellow recycling bucket and turned to go.

"I think it might be better if you left that here in my office, for safekeeping," Mr. Roemer said with what was clearly a wink. "You can pick it up after the 3:18 bell."

"Okay," Dinah said. She had done enough electioneering for one day. Maybe more than enough.

"Good luck with the election," Mr. Roemer called after her as she went.

"Thank you," Dinah called back. She meant it, too. She *liked* Mr. Roemer. She might even stop clearing her throat every day when the public-address system clicked on for morning announcements.

"On your *head*?" Mrs. Kelly asked in amazement. Dinah was glad to demonstrate. "Like this."

Suzanne's brother Tom gave a low whistle. "Watch out, Dynamite. You may have started a whole new fashion trend."

"And I just stood there, like for three minutes, until everybody stopped eating and talking and just, you know, stared at me."

"She really did," Suzanne put in.

"Then Artie Adams said, 'What's wrong with your head?' and I said, 'Nothing. What's wrong is that JFK Middle School has no recycling program, none at all.' "

"Hear, hear!" Tom said. "Did the multitudes burst out cheering when you finished?"

"Some people did. Not the boys. Especially not Jason Winfield. He called me Bucket Head. And then the cafeteria monitors made me go to the office."

Dinah finished the rest of the story. "So, what I want to know is, do you think this will make people vote for me, or not?" The point of the bucket stunt, after all, had been to win votes, not just to enjoy the delicious moment when the entire middle-school cafeteria had been struck silent by her entrance.

"I would think so," Mrs. Kelly said. "I've heard it said that all publicity is good publicity."

"Aw, you'll win," Tom predicted in the same breezy way that he had predicted the renaming of the school in Dinah's honor.

Their confidence reassured Dinah. Of course she would win. She could hardly imagine herself as an also-ran, sitting unnoticed in the bleachers at soccer games, while the crowd cheered instead for Blaine or Jason.

"Greg took a poll in our social studies class, after lunch today," Suzanne said hesitantly.

Much as Dinah wanted to ignore any mention of Greg, this time she had to ask, "And?"

"And it turned out, well, ten for Jason, seven for Blaine, and seven for you."

"Seven?"

"You and Blaine are sort of splitting the girls' vote."

"Seven." Dinah repeated the number numbly. "Then . . . I lost."

No. Dinah was *counting* on being class president. She had to be president, she just *had* to be. How else was she going to be a big frog in the big pond of middle school? There was the Drama Club play, but in fifth grade Dinah had learned the hard way that the best parts didn't always, necessarily, without exception, come her way. Dinah didn't want to spend the rest of her first year in middle school being one more nameless, faceless sixth grader. She wanted to be president of all sixth graders.

The thought of having victory snatched from her grasp by an unthinking block of boys voting against her made Dinah's temples throb.

"Greg probably set it up so that Blaine and I would lose," Dinah said. "He probably asked people: 'You don't want to vote for a *girl*, do you?' "

"Dinah!" Suzanne sounded almost angry.

Dinah felt herself blaming Suzanne, too. "Who won his poll for secretary? I bet you did."

"Well, as a matter of fact—"

"See? I knew it. If you two love each other so much, why don't you just go ahead and get married?"

"Aw, come on, Dynamite," Tom said. "Greg sounds like a good kid."

"You *would* think so. You're one, too."

"One what?"

"A boy."

"So?"

Dinah was losing patience—with Tom, with Suzanne, even with Mrs. Kelly, who stood quietly chopping onions on the butcher block next to the sink. Hadn't they noticed that Greg's poll predicted that she, Dinah, would lose the election? Lose it to a *boy?* How, in those circumstances, could Dinah's best friend like a boy?

"Never mind," she said stiffly.

"But I do mind," Tom insisted. "What's wrong with being a boy?"

"Tom," Mrs. Kelly said, "would you hop in the car and run to the 7-Eleven? I'm afraid I'm out of eggs for the corn bread."

Evidently overjoyed at the chance to drive, Tom snatched up his mother's car keys and disappeared.

"Let's go to your house," Suzanne suggested without meeting Dinah's eyes. "Your mom should be home by now. It's been days since I've seen Benjamin."

"Okay," Dinah said. But as they walked in silence the three blocks to Dinah's house, Dinah felt a tight knot of fear clench itself in the pit of her stomach. For the first time she was worried, really worried, about losing the election. And it seemed somehow that she was losing Suzanne, as well.

Nine

"This is it," Dinah's mother told her Saturday morning as they drove together to Mrs. Briscoe's house. "Today is the first day of the rest of Mrs. Briscoe's organized life."

"You're all done?"

"Just about. The house is done, or as done as it's going to be. I've noticed that Mrs. Briscoe is slipping back into some of her old ways. Did you see that new newspaper pile growing in the pantry? But at least I've given her a clean, tidy house to do with as she will. All I have left is to finish organizing her support services. I'm setting her up with a grocery delivery plan, arranging for the library bookmobile to stop by on a regular basis, making a slew of doctors' appointments, things like that."

"Does this mean Mrs. Briscoe can stay at her house?" Dinah asked. She had to know for sure. "Her mean daughter isn't going to kick her out?"

"Oh, Dinah," her mother said, "Ruth Briscoe isn't mean. She just has her own life to live. I'm not even sure I blame her. And Mrs. Briscoe *is* getting a bit dotty. She never remembers where she puts things, or whether she's paid her bills or not. That's another thing; I have to figure out a system for reminding her to take her heart medication."

"So you did it! You really made it so that Mrs. Briscoe doesn't have to go to a nursing home."

"*We* did it. Your visits were important, too. Isolation is a terrible thing for older people—for anyone. Thank you for all your help, Dinah. I appreciate it, and I know Mrs. Briscoe does, too."

Dinah had a sudden thought. "But I'm not even halfway through the book. The most I can do today is Chapters Six and Seven, and there are five more chapters after that. I checked last time."

"It's not as if Mrs. Briscoe hasn't read *The Wind in the Willows* before," Dinah's mother pointed out.

"I know. But I should finish the book, at least. I mean, I kind of promised that I would. If I came sometimes just by myself, could Daddy give me a ride afterward, on his way home from the store?"

Dinah's mother leaned over at the traffic light and gave Dinah a quick kiss. "He'd be proud to do it," she said.

At Mrs. Briscoe's house Dinah's mother began making some phone calls, while Mrs. Briscoe and Dinah started in on the next chapter of *The Wind in the Willows*. The day was gray and cloudy, with a storm threatening, and it was cozy sitting in Mrs. Briscoe's

kitchen, hearing about the faraway English country-
side. Reading aloud from a children's book made
Dinah feel young and safe again, the way she used to
feel before middle school, years ago when her parents
would read her a bedtime story. Even though now she
was the one doing the reading, it gave her the same
feeling of closeness and comfort.

In Chapter Six, Toad escaped from the watchful
eyes of his animal friends, stole a motorcar, and landed
himself in prison. If Toad had been running for sixth-
grade president, he, too, would have paraded through
the cafeteria with a yellow recycling bucket on his
head, if recycling, rather than motorcars, had been his
passion of the moment.

"If Rat and Mole and Toad and Badger were all
running for president, who would you vote for?"
Dinah asked at the chapter's end.

"Badger, of course. Wouldn't you?"

"You wouldn't vote for Toad?"

Mrs. Briscoe laughed. "Not for president. Not for
dogcatcher, for that matter. But I admit the book
would be dull without him."

Dinah scuffed her heels against the chair rung. "I
don't know if I'm going to win my election. At school.
My friend Suzanne likes this boy Greg, and he took
a poll, and according to him Blaine and I are splitting
the girls' votes. Jason Winfield is going to win."

"Polls can be wrong, you know," Mrs. Briscoe said.
"I still remember the time Harry Truman was running
for reelection against Thomas Dewey. All the polls

showed Dewey far ahead. One newspaper was so sure Dewey would win that it went ahead and printed up its front-page headline: DEWEY DEFEATS TRUMAN. But when all the votes were counted, Dewey didn't win. I may forget what day the garbageman is supposed to come, but I'll never forget the picture of good old Harry Truman, holding that paper with DEWEY DEFEATS TRUMAN. plastered across the front of it, grinning to beat the band."

Dinah liked that story. She poured the last of the tea into her cup.

"Do you know how it is when you really want something," she asked, "so that your whole chest hurts inside when you think about it?"

"I do." Mrs. Briscoe patted Dinah's hand. "Believe me, I do."

Mrs. Briscoe must want to stay in her house that way, the same way Dinah wanted to win the election. Now Mrs. Briscoe was going to keep her home, thanks to Seabrooke Organizing, Incorporated. Maybe that was a sign that Dinah would get what she wanted, too.

"Would you do me a favor, Dinah?" Mrs. Briscoe asked then. "We were talking the other day about recycling my newspapers, and finding someone with another use for them. I've been brooding about my frog collection. If anything should ever happen to me, I'd want my poor froggies to be 'recycled,' too. Ruthie was never one for knickknacks and— It would break my heart if they were just thrown away. Could I tell her that you'd take them? I'd dearly love for you to have them, especially Mr. Toad, of course, but the others, too."

Dinah swallowed hard over the lump in her throat. "You really want *me* to have them? All of them?"

"There's nobody I'd rather give them to."

"I'd take good care of them," Dinah said in a rush. "I'd let Benjamin look at them, but I wouldn't let him touch them until he was all grown up, like eleven years old. And I'd keep them in a special place, and dust them every week, and never let them get broken."

"I know you would," Mrs. Briscoe said. "But play with them sometimes, too."

"I will," Dinah promised.

"This is the best kind of recycling, don't you think? Passing on something you love to somebody you care about."

Two hours later Dinah sat on Mrs. Briscoe's front steps, caught up in the glow of Chapter Seven, waiting for her mother to finish, waiting for the storm to come. The sky was low and dark, swollen with rain that would fall any minute. It was perfect weather for dancing on a rooftop.

The wind blew through the weeds and wildflowers that had long ago taken over Mrs. Briscoe's patchy lawn—blue bachelor's buttons and goldenrod and Queen Anne's lace. Dinah decided to pick a big bouquet of flowers for Benjamin. She knew Mrs. Briscoe wouldn't mind.

A group of high-school kids came out of the library across the street and headed her way, talking and laughing, hurrying before the rain. As they passed Dinah, one of them wadded up a candy-bar wrapper and, without looking, tossed it into Mrs. Briscoe's yard.

He obviously didn't realize that Dinah was the environmental candidate for sixth-grade president.

"Hey!" Dinah snatched up the candy wrapper and ran after him. "Hey, you dropped something!"

The boy turned around to see what he had dropped. When he saw the candy wrapper, he shrugged. "So?"

"So that was somebody's *lawn*. That was my friend's lawn."

"Tell your friend to get some weed killer."

Dinah stood her ground. "Here. Take it."

Scowling now, the boy took his wrapper. "The grass on this side of the sidewalk belongs to the city," he said. "It isn't anybody's lawn." With exaggerated care, he set the wrapper on the narrow strip of grass between Mrs. Briscoe's front sidewalk and the street. "Okay?"

"No, it's not okay. Hey, you, come back here!"

But the boy and his friends were gone. One big raindrop splattered on the pavement, and then another. Dinah couldn't remember when she had been so angry. That boy really thought the whole world was his own personal trash can. She stuffed the wrapper into her jeans pocket, to throw away at home, or better still, to find some way of recycling.

In that moment, standing there on Mrs. Briscoe's sidewalk, with the rain pelting down all around her, Dinah knew that she had to win the election, not just to be the biggest frog, but to make the recycling program really happen.

She turned her face up toward the sky and let the rain run down her closed eyelids, her nose, her chin. Planet Earth needed her to be class president. That was all there was to it.

Ten

Benjamin was crawling. The Seabrookes spent most of Sunday afternoon out in their backyard watching him inch his way forward across an old quilt spread on the grass.

"Of course, it's not true crawling yet," Dinah's mother explained to her. "With true crawling he'd be up on his hands and knees. This is what you'd call creeping."

"But it counts," Dinah said. "For his baby book."

"You bet," her father said. He crouched down at the edge of the quilt. "Come on, little guy! Come to Daddy."

With a big, drooly smile, Benjamin headed over to his father. He propelled himself with his elbows, like an infant Marine dragging his way across a patchwork jungle.

"Way to go, Benjamin!" His father grabbed him up for a tickling hug, then set him down on the quilt again.

"Okay, Benjamin." Dinah took the next turn. "Come to me. Come to Dinah!" Sure enough, he crept in her direction.

Dinah was happy. For no reason at all, she was happy. Maybe it was the autumn sky, the newly washed blueness of it, bright and hard like the glaze on a porcelain bowl. The maple tree in the Harmons' yard was beginning to turn color, catching fire at the tips of the branches. The sun was warm, but the breeze had in it the sharp freshness of fall, Dinah's favorite season.

"I love the world," Dinah told Benjamin, flopping down on the quilt next to him. "Do you know how lucky you are to live here? In a world like this?"

"It'll do," her father said.

Flat on her back, Dinah gazed up at the sky. Maybe if more people lay on the grass and looked up, they wouldn't want to turn their world into a giant landfill. Or litter, or pollute. When Dinah was a famous actress she would use her fame to help environmental causes. She'd make television commercials for recycling, and people would say, "If a big movie star like Dinah Seabrooke believes in recycling, maybe we should, too." And if she were elected president of the United States someday, she'd make a law that everyone had to recycle, and she herself would use recycled paper for the invitations to her inaugural ball.

Dinah sat up. "The election is this coming Friday," she said. "That's just five days away. We'll have the debate in social studies on Wednesday, but only twenty-five people will be there to hear it. I have my two-minute speech at the assembly on Thursday, but two minutes isn't very long. I have to do something else, one more thing, so that every single sixth grader will know how much our school needs a recycling program."

"I suppose you could try wearing one of our trash cans on your head," Dinah's father suggested.

"Daddy! You're not being serious. I can't wear anything else on my head. It's against the dress code." All Dinah needed now was to be nicknamed Trash Can Head. Besides, wearing the bucket on her head hadn't really made the others understand anything about the importance of recycling. It had been a publicity stunt for Dinah herself, rather than a serious demonstration of the merits of her platform.

"I think you're doing enough," her mother said. "Your speech is sure to be wonderful, if I know my daughter."

That much was true. Dinah had already begun practicing her speech, and in her opinion it was every bit as good as Lincoln's Gettysburg Address. But the nagging doubts raised by Greg's poll refused to go away.

"No," she said. "I need one more thing."

Her parents exchanged glances.

"If you say so," her mother said. "But try not to get into any more trouble."

"I'll try," Dinah promised. But sometimes, despite her best intentions, trouble just *happened*.

*   *   *

On Monday morning, Dinah took the box of big plastic trash bags from the kitchen drawer and tucked it into her backpack. She had a plan. She'd stay after school and collect all the wastepaper thrown away that day, or as much of it as she could, and she'd carry it around with her throughout the day on Tuesday. Not on her head, just in a couple of trash bags she could drag behind her as she changed classes. *Look,* she'd say, *all of this was thrown away in one single day.* What more clear and dramatic way of showing the need for a schoolwide recycling program?

As soon as the 3:18 bell sounded, Dinah darted from room to room, eager to empty as many wastepaper baskets as she could in an hour. After half a dozen classrooms, her first trash bag was full almost to bursting. She left it next to her locker and started on another. In a few minutes, the second bag was full, as well.

On she raced down the long, silent halls of JFK Middle School, dumping basket after basket into her bags. The janitors would be surprised to find that some elf had arrived before them and spirited all the trash away.

By a quarter past four, Dinah was exhausted. She would never have guessed it was so much work to empty one school's trash baskets. Nor had she guessed one school could produce so much trash. Ten bulging sacks full of wastepaper stood in front of her locker.

Now what? Suddenly Dinah realized a fatal flaw in

her plan. She couldn't fit even one trash bag into her narrow locker, let alone ten. There was no way she could haul all ten bags home with her on the crowded bus. But if she left them by her locker overnight, the janitors would cart them away.

"Curly Top!" Dinah turned to find Miss Brady staring down at her. "What on earth do you have in those bags?"

Pirate's treasure. Canned goods for the needy. Freshly washed gym wear. Dinah rapidly ran through a series of lies, then said in a voice that came out smaller and squeakier than she meant it to, "Trash."

"And what, may I ask, are you doing with ten bags of trash?"

Wearily, Dinah explained. How many points would Brady take off for unauthorized trash collection?

"Where do you think you're going to put them now that you've collected them?" Brady's voice kept jabbing at Dinah like a long, bony finger. "I don't suppose you thought of that, did you?"

"No," Dinah admitted. "I was thinking about it just now, when you found me."

"Well, how about the gym locker room?" Brady suggested crisply. "There's plenty of room there. I'll leave a note for the cleaning staff not to remove them. You can stop by and pick them up first thing in the morning."

Dinah's eyes widened. She opened her mouth and then shut it again.

"Well, don't stand there gaping like a goldfish,"

Miss Brady snapped at her. "Let's take them there before you miss the 4:30 bus."

Brady hoisted four of the bags, two in each hand, and strode down the hall with them. Dinah made herself follow with another two. Together they came back to collect the rest.

"You'd better go now," Brady told Dinah when all ten bags were lined up against the rear wall of the gym locker room. "Mind you, I want these out of here by the start of first period tomorrow, no ifs, ands, or buts."

"But—" Dinah had to know. "Why are you helping me?"

"You think you kids are the only ones who care about recycling?" Brady asked. "I think it's a crime what this school throws away. I've said so time and time again at faculty meetings."

"What happened?"

"Nothing. Maybe something will now. I doubt it, but it's worth a try. Okay, Curly Top, out of here."

"Thank you," Dinah managed to say.

Brady brushed it away with the back of her hand. "Go!" she boomed.

Dinah dashed for the bus.

The next morning Dinah ran to the gym locker room as soon as the school doors opened. Miss Brady helped her tie the bags together with the thick twine Dinah had brought from the utility room at home. Then, dragging the bags behind her like a mule pulling a barge down the Erie Canal, Dinah made her slow, laborious way to homeroom.

No one had noticed when Dinah caught her skirt in her locker door the first day. But everyone noticed someone pulling ten trash bags down the hall. They had to notice, or they'd trip and go sprawling.

"Hey, kid, get out of my way!" an eighth grader shouted at her. But he was the one who ended up getting out of the way.

Luckily Dinah had thought to hang a sign around her neck, so she didn't have to waste any precious breath on explanations.

THIS TRASH WAS COLLECTED
IN ONE DAY AT YOUR SCHOOL.
SHOULDN'T IT BE RECYCLED?
DINAH SEABROOKE SAYS YES!

DINAH SEABROOKE

FOR SIXTH-GRADE PRESIDENT!

"Dinah Seabrooke for sixth-grade janitor!" one boy jeered, but Dinah was too tired to respond. The hall stretched out before her endlessly. *Bumpity, bumpity, bumpity, bump.* She dragged her load up the long flight of middle-school stairs.

Another boy chanted, "Jason's in the White House, waiting to be elected. Dinah's in the garbage can, waiting to be collected!"

Very funny. On Dinah trudged, pulling the weight of the world behind her.

Homeroom at last. Dinah left her load just outside the door and sank into her seat.

"What do you have in those bags, Seabrooke?" Jason asked her. He paused, obviously trying to think of a hilarious answer to his own question. Then his face lit up. "Deodorant!" he said loudly. "Dinah just bought a week's supply of deodorant!"

"Oh, shut up," Blaine told him. Blaine? "At least Dinah cares about something. At least there's something she *believes* in."

"That's right, Dinah believes in deodorant!" Jason was laughing so hard he had trouble getting the last word out.

"You are so juvenile, I can't believe it," Blaine said. "Just ignore him, Dinah."

Dinah threw Blaine a grateful smile. These days she was certainly receiving assistance from unexpected quarters.

"No," Mr. Prensky said as Dinah began dragging her ten trash bags down the aisle to her seat. "No. I won't stand for it. No."

"No, what?" Dinah asked, but she knew.

"I will not permit you to disrupt this class another time with your ridiculous campaign, or whatever you call it."

"I'm just trying to save the planet," Dinah said coldly.

"Well, go save it in Mr. Roemer's office. Go. Now."

Dinah obeyed. She and her trash bags made their grand exit from first-period English.

"You again," Mr. Roemer said when the secretary ushered her into his office. "What is it this time?"

Dinah told him.

"I thought we had agreed that you weren't going to cause any more disturbances," Mr. Roemer said.

Dinah doubted that she had agreed to any such thing. When Dynamite Dinah was around, disturbances were only to be expected. And this time was different. How were people going to realize the enormity of the trash problem in their school if Dinah didn't make them actually *see* how much trash there was?

"I didn't wear anything on my head this time."

"I suppose we can be grateful for that," Mr. Roemer said. He studied the ten trash bags. "You really collected all that paper in one day?"

Dinah nodded. "This isn't even all of it."

"Well, if one of this year's class officers wants to take the initiative for a recycling program, I guess I'd look into it."

Dinah's heart soared. If Mr. Roemer looked into a recycling program, he'd have to see what a good idea it was. Now all she had to do was get herself elected president so that he'd look into it.

"All right, Dinah, go sit out by Mrs. MacDonald's desk for the rest of the period."

"What about my bags?"

"You'll have to leave them here."

"But I *need* them. People *should* be disturbed by them. I *want* them to be." Dinah's rush of joy was perilously close to becoming misery.

"Look," Mr. Roemer said, "suppose we leave them outside the main office, just for today, with your sign taped to the wall next to them. How would that be?"

"That would be wonderful." Dinah thought about hugging Mr. Roemer, but decided against it.

He walked to the door with her. "Remember, Dinah, the squeaky wheel may get the most grease, but it doesn't necessarily get the most votes."

But Mr. Roemer didn't understand. Dinah had to get the most votes. She just had to.

Eleven

"Kids!" Mr. Dixon bellowed at the start of sixth period on Wednesday afternoon. "Clear your desks! Clear your minds! Today's the day we've been waiting for. Illustrious candidates, take your places."

Mr. Dixon set three chairs at the front of the room, facing the rows of desks. Dinah picked the chair farthest from Mr. Dixon. She liked to go last when she had a presentation to make. The last speech had the greatest impact.

"Each candidate will give a two-minute speech, then each will get two minutes to respond to the speeches made by the others. After that we'll open the floor for questions. Winfield, you're on."

Jason stood up. He looked tan and athletic and sure of himself.

"Why should you elect me president of your class? Because I have a proven record of leadership in sports. I was captain of my youth-league baseball team last year, and it came in second in the whole city. Being a team captain taught me a lot about getting along with people and getting them to work together toward a common goal. I learned how to make hard decisions and how to stick by them afterward.

"Right now I'm on the football team, and I'm the only sixth grader who's gotten to play in a game so far this fall. I plan to go out for the basketball and baseball teams, too.

"My dad says that sports are like life, and life is like sports. Don't you want a *winner* to lead your class as president? If you elect me as president, I'll work hard all year to turn JFK into a school of champions."

Some of the boys began to cheer, but Dixon rapped on his desk with the pointer. "Hold your applause. You'll get your say at the polls on Friday. Yarborough."

Blaine took her place. She looked pale, but composed.

"The greatest problem our school faces today—" Blaine paused for emphasis "—is apathy. A lot of people in this school just don't care about their schoolwork, about extracurricular activities, about their *school*. Less than half of all sixth graders attended the activities fair in September, and of those who did attend, less than half joined any club.

"The right to attend JFK Middle School goes hand in hand with certain responsibilities. Responsibilities to study, to obey school rules, to support school activities. There won't *be* any school activities unless we, the students, support them. No sports." Blaine nodded at Jason. "No Environmental Action Club." She nodded at Dinah. "No drama or music, no science fair, no school newspaper.

"Our school is named after the thirty-fifth president of the United States, John Fitzgerald Kennedy. In his inaugural address, Kennedy said, 'Ask not what your country can do for you; ask what you can do for your country.' I say, 'Ask not what your school can do for you, but what you can do for your school.' Get involved. Join a club. Try out for a team. Make a difference. All of us working together can make JFK the best school in the state. I'm ready. Are you?"

Blaine sat down. It was all Dinah could do not to burst into applause herself. Blaine made Dinah feel proud she had joined the Drama Club, guilty she hadn't joined the Environmental Action Club, sorry she had ever made fun of the Girls' Athletic Association. *Ask not what your school can do for you; ask what you can do for your school.* Dinah could have used a line like that herself: Ask not what your planet can do for you; ask what you can do for your planet.

"Seabrooke. Earth to Dinah Seabrooke," Dixon called out.

Dinah jumped. It was her turn. She walked slowly to the same spot where Jason and Blaine had stood. Then she began.

"I stand before you today as the only candidate for

sixth-grade president who will bring a recycling program to your school. Every person in this country throws away four hundred and eighty-one pounds of paper every year. Every day in this country, thousands of trees are chopped down to make paper, thousands of living, breathing, growing trees. Every day more acres of land become a landfill—a garbage dump, crammed full of waste that could have been recycled, that *should* have been recycled.

"The average school throws away tons of paper every year. On Monday I collected ten whole trash bags full of paper other kids had thrown away.

"Look," Dinah said. "Look around you. Lie down on the grass under a tree and look up at its branches. In spring they're covered with fragrant flowers; in summer with cool, green leaves; in autumn with fiery foliage; in winter with soft, white snow. It makes me sick to think of cutting down a beautiful, magnificent tree to make a bunch of Dittos." Scattered applause. "A tree is like a poem. Or a prayer. Or a symphony. It deserves to be saved, and loved.

"We have a chance to keep our planet green and growing. We can chop down more trees and dig more landfills, or we can save trees and recycle. The choice is ours. The choice, this Friday, is yours."

If that didn't make them want to save trees—and vote for Dinah—nothing on earth possibly could.

"Rebuttals. Winfield, two minutes."

Jason faced the class. "I don't really disagree with

anything Blaine said. Nobody's more involved in school activities than I am. But I can't go along with Dinah's big thing about saving trees. First of all, even if we recycled paper, nobody else does. If there're a million schools, and one recycles paper and the rest don't, I don't see how that helps anything. Besides, that's what trees are *for*—to use to make things people need. As far as I'm concerned, recycling is a dumb waste of time. About as dumb as wearing a bucket on your head to the cafeteria."

Jason grinned at Dinah. She made herself wait for her turn to reply.

"Yarborough."

"Jason tells us that *he's* involved in school activities. Good. I congratulate him for setting that example. But we need a president who's not only involved himself but will try to get others involved, too. And I want to see kids getting involved not just in sports, but in every school activity.

"Including recycling. Recycling is *not* dumb. I think Dinah's absolutely right about the need for a recycling program in our school. I would have made it part of my platform, except, well, Dinah thought of it first, so it belongs to her. But if I win, I will work to set up a program like Dinah talked about. *We* can do what's right even if everybody else doesn't."

"Seabrooke."

Dinah leaped to her feet, still as furious as she had been two minutes ago.

"What's dumb isn't wearing a bucket on your head. What's dumb is laughing at someone who's trying to make a difference. What's dumb is littering, and throwing away things that could be recycled, and cutting down trees instead of planting new ones. What's dumb is not even noticing that we've just been given one planet, and one chance to take care of it."

Dinah struggled to pull herself together. She wanted to say something as nice about Blaine's speech as Blaine had about hers. She took a deep breath and went on.

"Blaine is right. We *can* make a difference, in all kinds of ways we don't even dream about. Blaine's right that we should ask what we can do for our school. And what we can do for our school is set up a recycling program. What we can do for our planet is save it."

Dinah sat down. Her hands were shaking and she felt close to tears. But she had said what she wanted to say.

"Class. Questions. One at a time. Levine."

"This is for Blaine. I mean, it sounds good to get people involved in school activities, but how are you actually going to do it?"

Blaine had her answer ready. "I have a couple of ideas. One is that I think a different activity should be featured every week on morning announcements. That same week there can be a display all about that activity on the bulletin board in front of the main office. The school newspaper can print more stories about some of the clubs kids don't know much about, instead of writing all the time about sports. And sometimes kids should get out of class to work on a club activity. Everybody wants to get out of class, right?"

The others laughed. Then Mr. Dixon called on the next kid. "Foster."

"This is for Jason. Can you give us any specific example to show how being in sports has given you leadership experience?" Alex Foster was a friend of Jason's; they had obviously planned the question together.

"Good question," Jason said. "Here's one. When I was captain of my baseball team last year, the coach and I had to make decisions about which kids would get to play and which kids would have to sit on the bench. Sometimes good friends of mine ended up sitting on the bench, but I couldn't let them play just because they were my friends. I had to do what was best for the team. If I were president of our class, it would be the same way. I'd do what was best for everybody."

"Adams."

"This is for Dinah." The smirk on Artie's face gave the question away before he even asked it. "In general, do you like to wear strange things on your head?"

"Let's not waste time with jokes, Adams," Mr. Dixon warned.

"Okay, I have another question. Dinah, is it true

you love trees so much you want to marry one?"

"Okay, Adams, out of here. One chance is all I give."

Artie cheerfully collected his things and left for Mr. Roemer's office. But the damage was already done. Dinah felt her cheeks flaming. She'd certainly rather marry a tree than a boy.

"Does anyone have a *serious* question for Dinah?"

One girl put up her hand. "Do you really think you can get the school administration to adopt a recycling program?"

"Mr. Roemer told me himself that if one of the new officers took the initiative for a recycling program, he'd look into it."

It was a good answer. But Dinah could tell most kids weren't listening. From somewhere in the back of the room she heard again the familiar chant, "Dinah's in the garbage can, waiting to be collected!"

There were a few other questions, all for Blaine and Jason. Then Mr. Dixon rapped on his desk again. "That's it for today, folks. With the exception of our dear departed friend, Mr. Adams, you came up with some great questions. In the last U.S. presidential election, less than half of the eligible voters chose to exercise their right to vote. I hope all of you vote on Friday. It's up to you to choose one of these three candidates to lead your class through this academic year."

Silently he tapped the pointer against each of the

three names he had written on the chalkboard at the beginning of the class period.

Winfield.
Yarborough.
Seabrooke.

"Which one will it be?"

Twelve

Dinah let the school bus leave without her that afternoon. She had to recover from the debate before she could face the boys' teasing, even before she could face Suzanne's well-meaning questions. Dinah had done her best in the debate. In her opinion she had given a magnificent and dazzling speech that should have convinced even the desks and chairs in the classroom to elect her president. But the kids in her social studies class had been plainly unimpressed. Blaine had impressed them, as she had impressed Dinah. But Dinah couldn't shake the feeling that victory would go to Jason Winfield. It was preposterous, it was impossible, it defied belief—but, with Dinah and Blaine splitting the girls' vote, it looked as if it were nonetheless going to happen.

How would Dinah live through a whole year of middle school in which someone else was president?

No. She had to win, somehow, some way, despite what looked like the odds against her. She would be like Harry Truman. The *JFK Herald* would have its headline printed up: WINFIELD WINS. And then the votes would be counted and it wouldn't be Jason Winfield at all, or Miss Perfect, either, but Dinah Seabrooke, the girl who was sometimes too disruptive, sometimes too emotional, but who made other people care about trees. The outcome of the election depended on her speech tomorrow, and maybe on a miracle, as well.

Dinah started walking aimlessly down the sidewalk in front of JFK, scuffing through the dry leaves that were beginning to fall from the tall oaks arching over the school's well-trampled lawn. But after the first block, she knew where she was headed. She was going to see Mrs. Briscoe, not because it was her job, not because she had chapters of *The Wind in the Willows* yet to read, but just because she wanted to. She wanted to sip lemony tea and eat buttered toast as she poured out all her election woes to a wise person who seemed to understand her so well. It came to Dinah with sudden force that Mrs. Briscoe, odd and old and disorganized, had become her *friend*, the first real friend Dinah had made in middle school.

Helping Mrs. Briscoe to stay in her house had given Dinah something to feel proud about. In a small way, she had made a mark on the world. She had made a difference in somebody else's life. Dinah's friendship with Mrs. Briscoe gave her one last surge of hope that she might be elected president, after all, and given the chance to make a big difference through the recycling program.

But when Dinah rang the doorbell, Mrs. Briscoe didn't answer. Dinah gave her time to move slowly from the kitchen to the front hallway, then rang again. Could she be at a doctor's appointment? She hadn't said anything about one last time, but she might have forgotten all about it until the Red Cross lady came to pick her up. It was past four o'clock, though, and Dinah remembered that her mother had tried to schedule Mrs. Briscoe's appointments early in the day. "Older people don't like to wait," she had said.

So where was Mrs. Briscoe?

Maybe Ruth Briscoe had stopped by to take her mother out for a drive. *Ha!* Ruth Briscoe didn't often make time to see her mother. Besides, it was a work day, and she'd be at her office downtown.

Dinah rang again. She held her finger against the bell, in case Mrs. Briscoe had suddenly turned deaf. She stood on tiptoe to peer through the little slit in the lace curtain covering the glass in Mrs. Briscoe's door. Would she see Mrs. Briscoe hurrying down the hall to greet her?

Dinah squinted through the glass again. Then a giant fist closed around her heart. In the shadowy darkness of the front hall, she saw Mrs. Briscoe lying on the floor at the base of the stairs, motionless.

She forgot to take her heart pills, she had a heart attack, she's—

Frantically, Dinah rattled the doorknob.

"Mrs. Briscoe!" she shouted. "Can you hear me? It's me! It's Dinah!" She shoved against the door with her shoulder, hard, but it didn't budge. "Mrs. Briscoe! Open the door! It's Dinah! Mrs. Briscoe, let me in!"

"What's the matter?"

Dinah turned to see Greg crossing the lawn from his house to Mrs. Briscoe's.

"It's Mrs. Briscoe. She doesn't move. I think she's—"

"Okay," Greg said. "Calm down." But he hardly sounded calm himself. "Let's call the rescue squad. My parents have a key to her house. We can get in to see if she's . . . all right."

Inside Greg's house, Dinah drew deep shuddering breaths as Greg dialed 911. Numbly, she listened to him give the information. Then Greg grabbed the key ring from the hook by the front door and sprinted back to Mrs. Briscoe's house with Dinah beside him. Greg fumbled with the keys. Finally, the door opened.

Dinah held back as Greg laid a shaky hand on Mrs. Briscoe's chest.

"She's breathing!" Greg announced triumphantly. "But her leg looks funny. Is there a blanket or something we can cover her with?"

Dinah ran to get the quilt from Mrs. Briscoe's bed. Gently she laid it over the old lady's still form.

"They're here," Greg said. Two rescue-squad workers leaped from the ambulance and raced up Mrs. Briscoe's front steps. Greg and Dinah sat outside in silence as the men examined Mrs. Briscoe.

"Broken leg," one of them reported a few minutes

later. "And a nasty blow to the head. But she's beginning to come to now. Which one of you found her?"

"Dinah did."

"But Greg was the one who called."

"You kids did a great job," the man said.

"She'll really be okay?" Dinah asked.

"You bet. But it'll take time. Old people's bones heal slowly."

"Can she stay in her house while she gets better?" Dinah had to ask it.

The man shook his head. "I don't know. I wouldn't think so. She'll probably be laid up in a nursing home for a couple of months. Hey, kid, take it easy. Nursing homes aren't so bad. Hey, kid— What's wrong with her?" he asked Greg.

Dinah was crying too hard to speak.

"They're friends," Greg said. He put his arm around Dinah's shoulders.

"No relation? We need to notify any relations."

"She has a daughter," Greg said.

"Ruth," Dinah made herself say. "Ruth Briscoe. My mother has her number. She'll call her tonight."

The man patted Dinah on the arm. "Don't take it so hard, kid. Like I said, you did great."

"Mrs. Briscoe'll be all right," Greg said. Dinah shook her head. "She really will."

But Dinah knew that nothing would ever be all right again.

* * *

"She must have gone upstairs to look for something and slipped on the stairs," Dinah's mother said at dinner.

"But why? We moved everything downstairs, didn't we?" Dinah asked. She pushed her plate away, the food half-eaten.

"Not everything. Most of what I thought she needed. And you know how forgetful she is. She may have gotten confused about the new arrangements."

"So it didn't do any good. Everything we did. It was all one big failure."

Dinah's father spooned a bit of strained carrot into Benjamin's gaping bird mouth. "Dinah," he said, "accidents can happen to anybody, young or old, organized or disorganized. No one can guarantee someone else's total safety."

"But the whole point was for Mrs. Briscoe to stay in her own house," Dinah said, "and now she's not going to."

"I'm not sure that was the whole point," Dinah's mother said. "I've always thought that being organized helps people feel better about their lives—more in control of what's happening to them. Organized people are often happier people. At least that's what I've found."

"Being stuck in a nursing home with a broken leg wouldn't make me very happy," Dinah said.

"Dinah," her father said, "we know you feel bad about Mrs. Briscoe, but there's a limit to how guilty the rest of us want to feel. You're done eating. Why don't you go off by yourself for a while? Ask yourself whether Mrs. Briscoe was better off or worse off because of knowing you. I myself think the answer to that one is pretty obvious."

Dinah laid her napkin on the table. She delivered her parting shot. "By the way, I pretty much lost the debate today," she said. "Stupid Jason is going to win the election." Just in case her parents still thought there was anything left in life to be glad about.

Upstairs in her room, Dinah started crying again. Before, at Mrs. Briscoe's house, she had cried for Mrs. Briscoe, who would wake up in a hospital room far away from her frog teapot and bookshelves and favorite black squirrel. Now she cried for herself, Dinah Seabrooke, who wouldn't be class president, after all, who couldn't even keep Mrs. Briscoe out of a nursing home.

So far in middle school, Dinah had run for class president and most likely lost. She had tried to help an old lady and failed. She had been the secret star, one time, of morning announcements. She had acquired a nickname: Bucket Head. Actually, she was probably the best-known sixth grader in the school. That was something. But not, in the end, all that much.

The thought surprised her. At that moment she was probably the biggest frog in the sixth-grade pond at JFK Middle School. But, oddly enough, it gave her no satisfaction. What mattered was that the two most important things she had tried to accomplish had both ended in failure: Mrs. Briscoe was going to a nursing home; the recycling program would never come to be. Right then it seemed to Dinah that it didn't matter so much what size frog she was, but what kind of pond she lived in. More than anything in the world, Dinah wanted Mrs. Briscoe to be happy. And now that she had come to care about the recycling program for its own sake, she wanted it to become a reality—even more than she wanted to be elected president of her class.

One person can make a difference. Dinah had believed that. In particular, she had believed that *she* could make a difference. But she had been wrong. In the end, she hadn't made a mark on anything or anybody.

Dinah must have fallen asleep, because the next thing she knew, her father was shaking her awake.

"Telephone, Dinah. For you. It's Mrs. Briscoe."

Dreading what she might hear, Dinah followed her father down the stairs. He handed her the receiver.

"Hello?"

"Dinah, it's Mrs. Briscoe." The voice sounded faint and far away, but like Mrs. Briscoe all the same. "They told me that you were the one who found me after my silly fall this afternoon. You and the Thomas boy next door."

"Are you okay?"

"The doctors tell me I will be."

"But . . . I want you to come back home again."

"So do I. And I will, in a few months. But, Dinah,

home is just the place where your friends are, you know, the people you care about, who care about you. So if you'll come to visit me at the nursing home sometimes, why, it'll seem like a real home then."

Dinah's father had his arm around her shoulders. She reached up and took his hand and squeezed it tight.

"It will?" she asked over the lump in her throat.

"It will. Remember, we still have a few more chapters to read about our friend Mr. Toad. But now the kind nurse here tells me it's time to go. I just wanted to thank you, Dinah, for today, and for all the other days, too."

"Oh, Mrs. Briscoe—"

"Good-night now, dear."

"Good-night," Dinah whispered.

Dinah's father hung up the phone for her.

"What did I tell you?" he said. "You made a difference in Mrs. Briscoe's life, a big difference, even if it wasn't the kind of difference you were planning on. See?"

And suddenly Dinah did.

Thirteen

The sixth-grade election assembly took place the next morning, fourth period, in the middle-school gym. The candidates sat on metal folding chairs behind the podium set up under the far basketball hoop. The other students sat on the floor in long rows, facing them.

Mr. Roemer gave a brief welcome, then introduced Miss McKay, the sixth-grade class advisor. She explained that each candidate for class office would give a two-minute speech, first the candidates for secretary, then for treasurer, vice president, and, finally, president. Within each category, candidates would speak in alphabetical order.

"For the office of class secretary," Miss McKay read from her list, "the first candidate is Suzanne Kelly."

Dinah clapped wildly. "Go, Suzanne!"

On her way to the podium, Suzanne glanced back at Dinah and gave a shaky smile.

Suzanne's speech was short and modest. "I'm running for class secretary because I want to help out this year in all our class activities. If there's work to be done, I want to help do it. I can't say that I think I'm better than anybody else, but I know I would work hard and do my best. I think I can do the job. And I want to do it. Thanks."

The three Katies spoke in turn. As the treasurer speeches began, the kids in the audience began to squirm and fidget. One two-minute speech sounded very like another, and Dinah had trouble telling the candidates apart. The vice presidential speeches dragged on next. Why would anybody want to run for vice president, Dinah wondered. She decided that some kids must want the fun of holding an office without having to do any real work.

"And now, for the office of sixth-grade president," Miss McKay read, "the first candidate is Dinah Seabrooke."

The other sixth graders applauded longer and louder than Dinah had thought they would. Maybe they were looking forward to one speech, at least, that wouldn't be boring.

Dinah stood at the podium for a long moment. Was she making a mistake? No. She had made her choice, and it was the right one.

"I stand before you today," Dinah began, "to announce that I am withdrawing from the race for sixth-grade president."

She paused to savor the collective gasp of surprise that ran through her audience.

"Why? you may ask. Why am I leaving the race?

Don't I care about my recycling program? Don't I care about the tons of paper this school throws away every year? Don't I care that beautiful forests are chopped down and beautiful meadows turned into garbage dumps?

"Yes. I do care. In fact, I'm leaving the race just because I care so much.

"Blaine Yarborough also supports a recycling program. If all of you who would have voted for me vote for Blaine, I know she'll win, and she'll be a great president, and she'll save as many trees as I would have saved. I'm leaving the race because I don't want to see someone elected who doesn't care about the environment, who doesn't believe that each one of us can make a difference to our planet.

"I believe one person *can* make a difference. So does Blaine. Each of you can make a difference—by what you recycle, by what you throw away, by how you vote tomorrow morning.

"Make a difference with your vote. Vote for recycling. Vote for Blaine Yarborough."

Dinah sat down, but the clapping and cheering and stamping went on for so long that Miss McKay motioned for her to stand up again. "Dinah?"

Dinah stood there for one last sweet moment, smiling through the tears that suddenly glazed her eyes. It was a thrilling business, withdrawing from an election. She wished she could withdraw from one every day.

After Dinah's speech, the other two were plainly

anticlimactic. Jason, too stunned to understand how two fateful minutes had changed his sure victory into a sure defeat, gave yesterday's same speech about his proven record of leadership in sports. Blaine began her speech by thanking Dinah for her support, which set off another round of prolonged cheers. And the resounding roar of approval at the end of Blaine's speech left no doubt about who would be the next sixth-grade president.

As soon as Mr. Roemer dismissed the assembly, a crowd of students formed around Dinah to congratulate her. But Dinah pushed through them to find Suzanne.

"Oh, Dinah!" Suzanne hugged her tightly. "You were wonderful. I'm so proud!"

"You were pretty wonderful yourself, Madam Secretary," Dinah told her. "Where's Greg?"

"Greg?"

"Greg *Thomas*. The boy you're in love with."

"I'm not in *love* with him, I just *like* him," Suzanne protested.

"Well, you know what?" Dinah asked. "I've decided I like him, too." She told Suzanne about Mrs. Briscoe's accident.

"So, anyway," Dinah said, "I want to find out if Greg wants to come with me to the nursing home to see her. And you, too, of course. After we're done celebrating your election, and Blaine's."

As Dinah and Suzanne made their way to the cafeteria, more kids stopped to tell Dinah how great her speech had been. Dinah hoped the drama coach was taking notes, gathering helpful information on who would make a show-stopping Lucy or Snoopy in *You're a Good Man, Charlie Brown*.

She knew that by next week her speech would be forgotten. Next week Blaine, and not Dinah, would take office as sixth-grade president. But today was her day, her brief, shining triumph.

"Do you think there ever *will* be a middle school named after us?" she asked Suzanne.

"No," Suzanne said. "Do you?"

Dinah reached up and took one of her campaign posters down from the wall. She was about to throw it away, but remembered: It could be recycled. She'd save it in her locker until Blaine's recycling program was under way.

"I guess not," Dinah said. "But maybe someday." Anything was possible.